SOOT DEVIL

Books by Charles Geer

Dexter and the Deer Lake Mystery
Soot Devil

SOOT DEVIL

By Charles Geer

Illustrated by the author

A W. W. Norton Book

Published by

Grosset & Dunlap Inc., New York

For
Smitty

Library of Congress Catalog Card Number: 76-130849
ISBN 0-448-21405-9 (trade ed.)
ISBN 0-448-26176-6 (library ed.)
Copyright © 1971 by Charles Geer
All Rights Reserved
Published simultaneously in Canada
Printed in the United States of America

SOOT DEVIL

1

THE CHIMNEY

THE inside of the chimney was dark as a grave. A cascade of soot fell about the boy as he wielded the brush and scraper of his trade. He slowly levered himself upward with his elbows and knees. A momentary relaxation of his flylike hold would send him plummeting to the stone hearth, 20 feet below.

It was September 25, 1777, in the city of Philadelphia. The chimney sweeps could hardly keep up with the work of cleaning the black maze of flues that honeycombed the city's buildings. They were intolerable nuisances—the filthy chimneys that caught fire. They spewed their sparks about, showering down on the city, setting fires that endangered lives and property—threatening the very city itself. The sweeps had to climb many of them, when their long-handled brushes and ropes could not reach the thick layers of soot.

Now the flue narrowed and bent to one side. The blackened boy, fighting down the beginnings of panic, squeezed past the constriction in a series of convulsive spasms. He rested for a time, his feet clinging to the bricks. He cleared his throat, lifted the edge of the stocking cap that covered his face and spat into the gritty blackness. He resumed his squirming climb and presently, looking upward through the coarse weave of his cap, he saw a glimmer of light.

The cindery figure emerged like a deformed growth from the chimney top, four stories above the cobbled streets of the city. He pulled back his cap and flung out the old cry, "Sweep-O!" Below, his master, ogling the kitchen girls from behind a nose grown large and purple from rum, would know he had done his work.

He sat like a raven in its roost and peered out over the City of Brotherly Love through teary eyes. The tears were from the soot, not sadness. He had finished with the sad tears long ago.

He looked across the crazily tilting sea of roofs and chimneys, past the brick buildings of the Quaker merchants on Front Street to the broad, glinting sweep of the Delaware River and the green of New Jersey beyond. He rubbed his elbows gently, bit off the remains of a torn fingernail, scratched about under his arms and legs. His thin lips turned up at the corners, and he patted the bricks.

"Aye—ye kin tell all yer friends ye wuz th' last o' th' lucky chimblys wot wuz corkscrewed by this pore soot devil."

Cursing softly, he wiped at the tears. His thoughts wandered back into the past. Aye, th' buckets o' tears he'd shed—enough t' float a fine man o' war. Dimly he saw again the jovial kidnapper's face, the sailor's garb, in a dim alley of a forgotten city in a forgotten land. He heard the promises: the lovely things he'd see, the sweets. "Jist come aboard, there's th' good lad! Ye'll have a pocketful t' take home fer yer mum an' sis too!" And then the hatch had slammed above him, and he never did see his mum or sis nor that land again. Aye, he'd been a wide-eyed little innocent.

Was it five winters ago? Or four? It was hard to keep count. He must have been about eight years old then. But he could remember clearly enough the ship's dark hold and the long sea voyage. When it was over at last he was dry eyed, ready for the worst the New World might offer. And it offered its worst soon enough, when it came to that.

The chimney sweep, remembering, smiled crookedly. The ship's cargo had included some of His Majesty's seven-year passengers—thieves, rogues, murderers—scraped from the dank dungeons of Newgate and Old Bailey and sent to America, to make room in the prisons for more such London lovelies. Aye. He'd learned a thing or two.

The captain had sold the lot, including the stolen lads and lassies, as indentured servants—bound to serve their new masters for seven years, the children until they were 21. And he didn't have trouble selling any of them—the peg-legged, the one-eyed, the dim-witted, the creaking, toothless ancients, or the eight-year-olds. The gentle people of Philadelphia fought like haggling fishwives to buy, for there was a shortage of workers in America. Who could be particular?

The sweep heard his master bang the kitchen kettle impatiently four stories below. He coughed and spat more of the chimney's soot on the roof slates. A fine tub he'd fallen into.

Ah, th' curse o' bein' small! Th' blasted sot o' a kettle banger had picked him right out fer th' trade. Called hisself a plasterer. Ha!

The blackened boy shifted his position in the chimneytop. It was an old one, and the move sent several loose bricks rattling down the slates, tumbling out of sight into the depths of the alley below. He narrowly avoided going down with them. The silence of their final fall ended with the sound of breaking glass, the whinny of a frightened horse, a string of curses and then the sounds of a runaway cart.

"Me wine! Me Madeira!" The shout came echoing up to the sweep.

Across the alley, almost at a level with the sweep, a buxom, red-faced harpy leaned out of a window, brandished a fat finger at him and yowled loudly to those below. "It wuz 'im—that soot devil there—wot throwed 'em. A purpose, too! Hughie, dearie, git 'im—another one o' them no good, thievin' lily-whites!"

More banging came hollowly up the chimney and the muffled words, "You, boy! Git down here!" Running feet and angry shouts sounded in the street.

The sweep looked over at the tormenting witch. He raised a fist to her, spat and flung out a string of oaths. Then he swung his head around to survey the city and its forest of chimneys. He threw his head back defiantly. His shout burst forth like a heady wine that had been bottled up too long.

"Sweep yer own mucky chimblys then—an' devil take ye!" And he disappeared down the flue like a genie.

2

GILLIGAN

PATRICK GILLIGAN called himself a master plasterer—which made it easier to get apprentices. The mums and dads and the Overseer of the Poor felt better thinking their little tots were learning a proper trade. He waited now in a state of great agitation to welcome the sweep back to the hearth. The giggling kitchen girls had fled from his leering eyes.

He lifted a corner of the gritty blanket hung from the mantel to protect the room from the soot. He could hear the fluttering, birdlike sound of the sweep descending. Poker held tight in a white-knuckled hand, he dropped the blanket and listened to the commotion in the street.

Blast th' little brush. It wuz hard enough, he thought, t' make a few shillin's without stirrin' up th' streets. An' no tellin' wot might happen in th' city o' Philadelphia these days. Everybody jumpy as cats—wot with th' British ready t' take th' city any day now. An' a good thing that would be too. Git a little law

an' order again! He swallowed and ran a yearning tongue around his lips. An' mebbe a nip o' decent rum, too.

Blast th' rebels! Givin' shillin' idees t' every tuppence boy. Stirrin' things up! He banged on the great black kettle and glowered up at the chimney. Apprentices were running away nearly every day. His face contorted in pain as he recalled the pounds and pence he had spent on advertisements in the *Pennsylvania Packet* for the return of his boys. Th' blasted injustice o' it. It wuzn't easy t' teach a new brush. Th' lily-livered new ones had t' be ruddy well stuffed up th' flue th' first times. Ah-h-h—ye couldn't be softhearted if ye wanted t' break 'em in right. Why, he'd pinched their bottoms, stuck pins in 'em, even built straw fires under 'em when they thought they wuz stuck—an' they'd got unstuck all right! Then, after all that trouble, in a couple o' years they git too big or git sick an' they're no use anymore.

He slashed at the air with the poker. A weak stock they wuz, not good fer anythin' better if they knowed th' truth. Always gettin' sick with somethin': consumption, cancers, chillblains, an' —— His thoughts were interrupted by the sound of the sweep landing lightly on the hearth.

The master plasterer moved quickly for a big man, but not as quickly as the boy who nimbly sidestepped as the poker hissed viciously through the air toward his shoulder. It whacked the blanket instead, sending up a cloud of soot. Mr. Gilligan coughed, cursed and then, at a sound behind him, stopped abruptly. Spinning around, he snatched off his greasy felt tri-corn, bowed and smiled as winningly as he could with his few remaining teeth.

"Yes Mam, all done, slick as a whistle—from th' bottom t' th' top. Ye'll not be havin' a spark or a flame out o' that flue. Ye'll be glad, Mam, that ye called on Patrick Gilligan. He has, if ye'll excuse his braggin', th' best brushes"—he beamed at the boy—"in Philadelphia an' is hisself, heh-heh, known fer his honest dealin's an' "—he lowered his eyes and proffered his palm—"his reasonable prices. That'll be one shillin' six, Mam, in hard money as agreed."

The mistress of the house, clothed in the long gray dress, cowled bonnet and gentle appearance of a Quaker listened with an air of distaste, a dainty linen kerchief at her nose. "If thee works at thy job half as hard as thee talks, I will be satisfied."

She dropped the coins into his grimy hand from a height, then moved on to the boy who stood on the hearth, black as a stick of charcoal, except for the whites of his bloodshot, blinking eyes and the muddy paths of the tears down his cheeks. He was clad, if one looked closely, in underclothes. She peered at him vaguely for a moment, dropped a penny in his hand, as was the custom, and then disappeared through the door murmuring, "What is that commotion out front?"

Quickly, under the baleful look of Mr. Gilligan, the sweep took down the blanket, swept the pile of soot in the fireplace onto it and tied it into a bundle. He put on his tattered leather breeches and patched coat. Gathering the blanket, brushes and scrapers, they stepped cautiously out of the door into the backyard of the house. Pausing there, Mr. Gilligan reached out with a practiced hand and twisted the sweep's skinny wrist sharply until the boy dropped the penny into his cupped and waiting hand. He nodded with satisfaction.

The irate shouts of the cart driver and his friends could be heard at the front door. The sweep and his master disappeared over the back fence and made swiftly for the next alley.

3

---◆---

THE STREET

M R. GILLIGAN, puffing hard as they turned onto crowded Walnut Street, slowed his pace. He thrust his flushed face within inches of the sweep's ear, which he held tightly between thumb and forefinger. The boy recoiled from the gusts of foul breath.

"Ye'll watch yerself"—gasp—"more careful next time laddie, loafin' an' throwin' bricks,"—gasp—"an', an' show a little gratitude! Like yer papers said, I've teached ye th' art an' mystery o' th' trade an' as long"—wheeze—"as there's a dirty chimbly in Philadelphia, or plasterin' work when times git better, ye've got work, an' straw, an' victuals."

He frowned as his eyes fell on the Statehouse, its tower rising above the surrounding buildings. He reluctantly released the ear. He forced a smile and squeezed a tortured wink at the boy. Ah-h, if this one ran away he'd be left with—let's see—that new one whose sore elbows an' knees hadn't calloused up good yet an' that one wot coughed blood all th' time now —th' ladies din't like that much—an' that one wot had found

11

kinfolk someplace who wuz bleatin' t' th' Overseer of the Poor
—who bye th' bye had been very happy t' git th' lout out of his
almshouse—about his not learnin' plasterin' like his papers
said. If he lost this here one—well, maybe he'd have t' git him
some o' those black pickaninnies who wuz takin' over th' trade.
He grinned. At least they couldn't run away so easy—spot 'em
quick. No big ideas an' nobody worried over them fer certain.
Have t' change with th' times—like a good businessman.

But still, fer wrigglin' up a flue quick this here monkey was
hard to beat. He reached, fumbling, into a leather pouch inside
his shirt and at last withdrew a penny. He paused for an
anguished moment—then held it out wordlessly to the boy,
who snatched it like a striking snake.

They hurried along the cobbled street, slippery with the
garbage and litter of a city with its mind on other things.
Groups of people talked nervously on street corners. Some,
laden with belongings, were clearly leaving the city. Occasional
brawls burst out raggedly. The clusters of people moved aside
however at the approach of the grimy sweep and his hulking
master. The acrid stink of the flues, a mixture of grease and
soot, enveloped them. Women gathered their skirts, be they
of fine silk or coarse homespun and drew back with distaste.

Three idling boys straggled along in the wake of the pair.
One of them reached down to a pile of garbage, and a moment
later something soft and slimy landed with a splat on the
sweep's back. He spun about, spitting curses. Gilligan grabbed
him and dragged him along. Another of the boys dashed up
to within a pace of the sweep and spat. The sweep broke free,

swung the blanket load of soot and caught the boy a blow on the side of his head before Gilligan roughly grabbed him again, shaking him like a dust rag. The boys laughed shrilly as they drifted off. "He tetched ye, he done tetched ye. An' now yer goin' t' turn into a soot devil! G'wan—git away from us—git. Ye be a stinkin' soot devil now."

Gilligan cuffed the sweep about absent-mindedly. Then the boy slung the soot back on his shoulder and fell in beside his master once more. His face was bent with half a smile.

A steady stream of mutterings from the master plasterer began again.

"An' ye'll notice," Gilligan mocked, pointing to the State-house, "that th' gintlemen o' th' brave Continental Congress has left, ye might say fer safer parts. Genr'l Howe is chewin' up them rebels like they wuz chickens an' spittin' out th' bones. Beat 'em at Brandywine—an' then he stuck 'em like pigs at Paoli tother day, and sure as my name is Patrick Gilligan, Sweep, he'll be here tomorra an' ——"

The sweep trotted on like a dog at heel beside its master. Sweep! He grimaced. He had a proper name—aye, he remembered the name—a name that he heard from out of that dim, distant past. Oh, there was a name on his indenture papers plucked out of the air by the ship's captain who had stolen him. But for years now it had been sweep, brush, soot devil, lily-white, boy, lad.

"——an' that'll be th' end o' Washington an' that bunch wot he calls his army," the master continued scornfully. "An' then ——"

The sweep shifted the load on his skinny shoulders. He remembered General Washington from that day he led the rebel army down Front Street. Drums and fifes playing. Every man with a piece of greenery on his hat on the way to fight the British. *Well,* he thought, *a whole lot o' good any o' them be t' me. Whatever th' fightin' be about it fer certain ain't about me! Aye, a rebel chimbly be as black as a tory chimbly fer all that.*

"——mebbe then," continued the plasterer, "a man kin collect his wits again and things'll settle down."

The sweep caught a glimpse of the river at the street's end and the hazy outline of New Jersey. He would have to hurry,

now that he had made up his mind. The odd pair turned from the confusion of Walnut Street and threaded their way through narrow streets and alleys toward that unsavory part of the city where Mr. Gilligan and his boys lived.

4

GILLIGAN'S PLACE

THE STUMP of a tallow candle flickered with an uncertain, greasy flame. Its foul smell mingled with the stench from the nearby tannery, and the other powerful odors floating about behind Mr. Gilligan's house. His boys also cleaned cesspools. It dimly lit the inside of the dilapidated shed where the sweeps slept. A small figure in the shadows sat up with a rustling of dirty straw and peered at the boy hunched over by the candle.

"Wot ye doin'?"

"Mendin' me pants, Half Pint, that's wot. Thought ye wuz asleep."

"Where'd ye git th' needle—steal it?"

The boy bent wordlessly to his task, squinting in the poor light.

"Ye goin' somewheres?" came the question from the straw after a pause.

"Where'd I be goin' 'cept up another bloomin' flue?"

There was heavy silence, and the white eyes bored out of

17

the darkness at the boy, who shifted uncomfortably on his stool.

"Why ain't ye out gamin' an' all like ye does with th' rest?"

The boy glanced at the other matted beds of straw, empty in the shadows. "Yer mouth jist flaps like a flag, Half Pint. Git back t' yer sweet dreams."

"Yer runnin' away aint' ye? I seen ye scrubbin' yer face, countin' yer money an' all." The voice took on a note of urgency. "Take me along. I can't go up them chimblys no more. Me elbows an' knees is bleedin' sore an'——hey wotcha doin'?" A boot flew across the shed and narrowly missed the side of his head.

The boy shot a look out of the door toward a dimly lit window of Mr. Gilligan's house, then turned to the small figure. "That be enough o' yer blubberin'. Wot d'ye think I be— daft? Go where? Ye ever seen wot happens t' runaways? Them sores would be th' nicest feelin' part o' yer bleedin' body." He picked up his things and flung them toward the straw, blew out the candle and lay down under the blackened blanket he had carried the soot in earlier. "Ye've got a lot t' learn Half Pint—ain't dried behind yer ears yet."

He sighed. The new boy was sniffling. "Ye'll git used t' it, Half Pint," he said gruffly. "Ye gits used t' anythin'." He felt a hundred years old. He rolled over onto his side and stared into the dark.

Get used to it? There was a joke. The boy whistled through his teeth. Every pound the tot put on would make the flue smaller and smaller. Not that he'd get exactly fat on the slops served here. Well, he for certain couldn't take anyone. Would be bad enough by himself. Nobody had ever looked after him. There were no soft hearts in this end of town.

He felt for his money pouch under his shirt. He had added a few pence on the sly that afternoon—beating carpets for some Tories who were sprucing up for the British.

His thoughts roamed ahead. He'd heard about the Pines from the Jerseymen. Farmers with produce to sell or fishermen who came to the city in the winter when their catch wouldn't spoil on the long wagon trip from the coast. And from some others around the city who knew where a body could hide if he had to.

The Pines was a fearsome, dark region to hear tell. It started about 20 miles from Philadelphia—the swamps, the bogs, the gloomy pine forest. They said it was like another world, like an island by itself, different from all that lay around it. It stretched all the way to the great bays on the coast. Little rivers snaked deep into the forest—hiding the rebel privateers, it was said.

"Methinks," he had overheard one Jerseyman burst out, "tis a wee bit o' hell right here on earth. And filled," he had added darkly, "with them as belongs in that place." Army deserters, thieves, murderers, brigands, smugglers behind every tree it seemed. And in the midst of the gloomy wilds, it was said, were the fires of hell itself—places where iron was made from the very earth.

The sweep smiled grimly. *Tis a proper soundin' spot fer th' likes o' me. None o' yer city streets fer this one.* Ah-h-, he'd seen the runaways dragged back from Burlington and Trenton. *Aye, th' witless wooden heads wot thinks a few miles an' a*

*different town is goin' t' do th' trick. Th' devil. That world be
fixed agin' 'em. It be th' same way, Tory or Rebel.* He pitched
over on his back. *'Course, wot with th' fightin' an' all it be
gettin' easier t' disappear—if ye has yer wits about ye.*

A loud bellow from Patrick Gilligan's window broke through
his thoughts: "An' ye'll git off th' streets an' quit yer caperin'
ye thievin' no goods."

Unsteady footsteps and giggling, poorly muffled voices approached the shed in the darkness. Racking coughs punctuated
one of the voices.

"So help me," said one, "I'm thinkin' t' stuff a cobble down
yer gullet if ye don't quit yer everlastin' coughin'."

"Shut yer face an' gimme th' jug." There was more loud
coughing.

Two dim shapes appeared in the doorway. One of them
lurched off into the blackness, away from the straw. "Darker
'n Gilligan's heart—whups! Where's me beautiful, downy bed?"

"I thinks yer goin' in th' wrong direction, mate," the other
giggled. He pointed shakily to the end of the shed. "I thinks
yer headin' fer the ——"

"If'n I don't know where me own bed is it be a sad —" A
violent string of oaths followed, and a moment later the second
figure reappeared in the doorway coughing and brushing himself and sending up a great dark cloud.

"Devil take it—why din't ye tell yer mate? Ye jist let him
walk right in t' th' soot bin. As if I din't git enough o' that!
Gimme back th' blasted jug. Wuz my winnins wot bought it."

There was a gurgling pause.

"Ah-h-h! Well, like I tole ye"—he smacked his lips—"I ain't

goin' t' be one o' Gilligan's corkscrews much longer." He snickered. "Aye, I found me old auntie in a grog shop on Water Street, an' she's goin' t' see th' Overseer gits me in a proper trade."

"Ah! Won't ye be fine an' grand! Wearin' fine silks an' laces an' velvet no doubt," crowed the other. "But me advice is t' not hold yer breath while yer waitin'."

Exchanging insults, they blundered to the straw and soon they had fallen heavily asleep.

The boy had quietly watched them. He lay on his back, staring, wide awake, hands clasped behind his head. Ah. There be th' end o' it all. They wuz 14, almost finished sweepin'— almost too big now fer climbin'—an' wot t' show fer it? One a sot, one with th' lung sickness—no trade, nobody 'bout t' hire a soot devil, but t' clean a cesspool maybe. There must be somethin' better a body could do with a life.

The first drops of rain began to splatter on the roof above his head. He watched the light in Mr. Gilligan's window and waited.

5

LEAVING

THE drenched boy stood pressed to the brick wall in the passageway that led from the alley to Gilligan's yard. The drumming rain had plastered his hair about his head, sluiced down his neck and soaked his clothes. He peered into the alley, then over his shoulder in the direction of the shed. From the window just above his head loud snores could be heard over the rain.

"Me best wishes t' all o' ye," he muttered under his breath, "an' sleep tight." He giggled mirthlessly. "I'm goin' t' find me bloody fortune." He stepped into the alley and scuttled hurriedly along the wet cobbles without a backward glance.

The sweep picked his way through the dark city as if he had developed the mysterious senses of a bat during his long service in the chimneys. He avoided the light like some pale, nocturnal animal. He used the ways he knew best—the sleazy alleys and crooked lanes where he and his sooty friends had roamed, caroused, played their mean games. No danger of Tory patrols here. They gave this part of town a wide berth.

22

At Front Street he paused warily. The fine brick homes, whose flues he knew so well, told him he was now on dangerous ground. The river lay down past Water Street, cloaked in the rainy mists.

Even through the rain the smells of the waterfront were there—tarry, spicy, pungent with the lingering odors of cargoes from mysterious, faraway islands. The big ships weren't at the docks now, driven to other ports by the British blockade. The streets were ominously empty, the noisy sailors' taverns quiet. Ah, but he could still see the sailors. Blackened by the sun, swaggering up to the taverns from the ships—their tarred pigtails, their dancing gold earrings, their wide flopping pants—a seabag or a chest on one shoulder and like as not a green parrot from the tropics on the other, raucously mimicking the curses of his master. And spenders! Flung their guineas and pieces of eight around as if there was no tomorrow, then sailed off again like carefree birds—flying free above the rest of the struggling world.

The sweep gave himself over completely to the picture, captured by the old dream. He stepped, unaware, out of the shadows and slowly walked along Front Street, his eyes seeing only the visions in his mind—hypnotized perhaps by the steady rhythm of the rain.

It was too late when he heard the splashing footsteps behind him. He was surrounded quickly by a dozen dark figures. From beneath the cloaks of several the dull gleam of pistol barrels could be seen. One who carried a lantern came forward and peered closely at him, the rain running in rivulets from his tricorn.

For a wild moment the sweep imagined that his scrubbing and the rain had cleaned his soot-pocked face, erased the sooty warts and sores, the signs of his despised trade.

"A Godless soot devil!" The man straightened and backed off. "Stinks like a slaver. Just the one who'd set the torch to our city."

The sweep hiccoughed expertly, swayed tipsily toward one of the men, who recoiled instinctively. He held out a cupped hand, "Hows fer a copper fer th' pore lil soot devil?" He reeled

about and pitched into the man and then fell sprawling on the wet cobbles. He played a part he knew well, a part expected of the likes of him. There was loud laughter.

"Th' little devil's drunk. Been dippin' his black bill."

"Been at th' spirits fer certain, th' little tosspot of a beggar. Look at 'im."

"Aye, he be in some other world fer fair."

One by one the glinting guns withdrew behind the cloaks. The man with the lantern lowered it to his side.

"Methinks we can best serve the king elsewhere. Treason is not on his fuddled mind. Let the little sot go back to where he came from, and may our good Lord have mercy on this poor wayward son."

The dark ring withdrew from about the boy, formed into a ragged black clot and moved off down Front Street. The sweep watched for a few moments, then got to his feet and darted down past Water Street to the river's edge below.

Half an hour later he leaned, exhausted, against the piling of a dock. There was not a skiff left on the river. The Rebels had picked the city clean to the bone before letting the British have it. He stared down at the dark, greasy river waters sucking softly back and forth, rhythmically thumping floating debris against the dock.

Shivering, he slid down against the piling until he sat huddled, hugging himself in the inky shadow at its base. He shut his eyes tightly, balled his hand into a fist. *Ah, yer a dim lamp fer sure! Wot d' ye expect—a fine bloomin' ferry with a red carpet an' a brass band?* He twisted around and looked up toward the faint lights of the city behind him. *Still time t' git back t' Gilligan's, crawl in t' th' straw an' wake up tomorra as if nuthin' had happened. It'll be a regular holiday an' mebbe* —he felt his little money pouch—*git a jug, an' later a game an' watch th' Lobsterbacks march in.* He rested his arms across his knees and laid his head down.

He sat motionless, the rain drumming relentlessly, as if it would wash him and the city into the river and out to sea.

After some time the sweep's head slowly lifted. He listened to the thumping sounds from below and thoughtfully stroked his chin. Presently he got to his feet and, leaning far out over the dock's edge, stared down at the water. He straightened and stood motionless. Then he removed his shoes and stuffed them into his shirt, wrapped his arms and legs around the piling and shinnied down toward the water.

His feet cautiously felt about, touched a rough log and tested it. He slid completely into the water and grasped one end of it. He kicked experimentally and the log carried him out from under the dock. He smiled and thought, *Don't go floatin' away or I'll sink like a cobble.*

He resumed his kicking and, after a time, when he looked back the city had disappeared behind a damp curtain of rain.

6

FRESH BREAD

THE RAIN had stopped at last. Now the sweep could see, against the dark sky, the darker outline of tall grass. He kicked weakly, and this time when he stopped his legs sank down and touched a stony bottom. He stood for a moment and watched the log turn lazily as the current carried it off into the blackness, and then he splashed toward the shore.

He collapsed, spread-eagled, his face resting on the coarse grass and mud. "Thought ye wuz goin' t' be fish food, I did." He rolled slowly over and flung an arm over his face. Presently he crawled forward, shivering, until he reached drier ground. He covered himself somewhat with the long grass, pulled his coat about and lay in a tight ball, hands between his drawn up legs.

When he awoke it was light. He sat up stiffly, cursing and muttering softly. "Ye waterlogged soot devil, ye feels cold as a corpse, ye does."

He knelt and peered over the top of the grass. His face broke into a grin and he nodded. Some distance upriver, on the far side, he saw the cluster of red-brick buildings that was Philadelphia. They thrust their chimneys into a clear blue sky. "Aye, soot devil, after pretendin' ye wuz a fine haddock all night, I be glad t' see ye landed on th' right side o' th' river!" He jumped up and down and rubbed his hands and flailed his arms to get warm. "Ye be a fair marvel of a sailor fer certain."

He turned and made his way through the woods that came close to the river here, and soon he stepped out of them onto a rough road. He walked north until he reached the small settlement opposite the city where the New Jersey ferries crossed the river. He cast a long, final look across the water, then turned and trudged along the narrow, rutted road that led east. He squinted gratefully at the morning sun and patted his clothes. They were almost dry.

By midday the farms had become fewer and the woods closed in about the road for long stretches. He scuffed along, peering about curiously. He picked up a fallen branch and whacked it noisily against a tree and shouted aloud, "Devil take th' bloody quiet!" He stamped his feet. "Nor any cobbles under yer feet." He grinned. "Comes t' that, ye daft soot devil, wot's a fine city boy like yerself doin' here with th' blasted savages?" He broke off a green twig and chewed on it for he was very hungry.

He continued on until midafternoon, his mind now completely occupied with his empty stomach, and when he saw the clearing of another farm, his face set with resolve. "If'n ye can't lighten their larder a bit, ye'd best jist crawl back t'

Gilligan's." The cabin came into view and he stepped to the fence and peered between the rails. His eyes narrowed, and his mouth hung open in puzzlement.

A man stood on the cabin roof, clinging to the stone chimney with one arm while under the other he held a struggling goose. On the ground a girl with flaxen hair wrung her hands and wept. The man leaned over the chimney and with some difficulty stuffed the white bird, loudly honking, down the flue, paying out a line as he did. A cloud of soot from its flapping wings rose from the chimney. Several times he pulled the weighted bird back up, then lowered it again. When he finally lifted the bedraggled bird clear it looked as if it had been dipped in an ink pot. His voice carried across the clearing.

"The blacker the bird the cleaner the chimney, me lass." He lowered it to the ground. Tearfully she embraced her sooty pet.

The sweep ran a soot-pitted hand through his hair. "A soot devil fer th' city chimblys an' a goose fer th' country ones," he said. He leaned on the fence rail and looked about—at the stout cabin, the fields, at the browsing cow, its bell softly tinkling. He heard the steady thump of a loom inside the house. He watched a boy gathering pumpkins in the field near the woods. "Aye, soot devil, it be purty as a picture. There be a sweet life fer sure."

Over it all, the smells of food hung in the air. Sniffing, the sweep's nose rummaged frantically about among them, savoring this and that. Meat pie made before cooling the chimney for the poor goose. And fresh baked bread too.

The sweep jumped over the fence and assumed a limp as he walked toward the girl. When she saw him, she jumped to her feet and the goose fled, honking and flapping. The girl was teary and soot-smudged but her wide, pretty face seemed friendly.

"Hullo. Who be ye?"

He shuffled to a halt. He let his shoulder sag piteously to one side, his head hung cravenly and his eyes fastened on hers like leeches. He started to thrust a beggar's hand forward. But—devil take it! Ah-h, she wuz a fair lass. Aye, it wuz a sweet face. He pulled back his hand and fumbled for the pennies in his pouch. "I wuz thinkin'," he straightened up somewhat and held out a copper, "I wuz thinkin' t' buy some victuals."

She gave him a curious look and called to her father. Then she turned back to the boy. "Ye looks worse'n a charcoal burner—an' yer a wee mite fer that fer certain."

The sweep clutched gratefully at the offering. "Aye—I be a charcoal burner. Me name"—he took a deep breath—"me name be Tom Fry."

The girl's father had clambered down the ladder. Grumbling, he brushed himself. "Black man's work it be." He straightened up and looked at the boy. His lips set themselves in a taut line. Then his voice grated harshly.

"A poor joke this be. A soot devil—a white soot devil from the city—and a runaway I have no doubt."

"Pa, he be jist a little mite."

He brusquely motioned his daughter into the house. "Little

or not—that's as may be, Sarah—but what he be is a thieving, capering, runaway soot devil." He turned back to the boy. "They be a bad lot. All cut from the same poor piece, they bring naught but evil and trouble."

The sound of the loom stopped, and his wife's face appeared in a window. His voice rose. "We be God-fearing, law-abiding folk here, and ye'll find no help from us in breaking your lawful bond, leaving your rightful master." He glowered down at the boy, who now began to slowly back away.

Then, abruptly, the farmer's expression turned thoughtful. He glanced back at the house and lowered his voice. "Ye'll have come from the city." He stroked his chin and appraised the boy. "Wait now. What be the news—have the British taken the town?" His eyes narrowed. "They'll be having hard money to buy my produce," he mused, half to himself. "Well, boy?"

The sweep stood silent for a moment. His eyes grew crafty, searched about and came to rest on the loaves of bread cooling on a window sill beyond the man.

"I be tryin'," he frowned in concentration, "t' git it in me mind jist wot wuz happinin' when I left th' city. It be fearsome hard t' remember—fearsome hard—wot with this an' that."

The farmer followed the boy's gaze to the bread—and then back to the faintly smiling face. He nodded grimly. The bargain was struck. "Aye! Aye!" he thundered, casting an eye to the house, "in the name o' sweet mercy and the Good Lord I'll feed ye—but mind ye, don't pass this house again."

Clutching two loaves of bread to his chest, Tom Fry gave the news from Philadelphia, with such bloodthirsty and lurid details about the British that the man's face turned white and his mouth dropped open. Smiling, the boy walked swiftly out of the yard and down the road. Not until he had reached the woods did he slow down and ravenously bite into the bread.

7

THE PINES

THE late afternoon sun streamed through the pine forest. The sweep kneeled in the shallow, tea-colored water of a small stream. He picked up another handful of sand from the bottom and rubbed it vigorously over his hands and arms. Most of his body was reddened from the scrubbing.

He washed the sand off and sat quietly in the softly flowing water. His wavering reflection looked up at him, and he shook his head dubiously and swore.

"Aa-a-ah—ye still looks an ugly, scrawny chicken ye do."

He turned his arms this way and that and examined the ground-in soot. All over his body his pores were black, and some had turned into ulcerous sores and ugly black lumps. He bent to study them, and his mouth twisted in disgust. "Aye—yer a fair beauty." Lumpy, dark callouses covered his elbows and knees. Beneath the soot and the redness from the sand lay an unhealthy, gray pallor. His fingers passed over his face, thin and pinched like his birdlike body. His ribs stuck out like a stray dog's.

He put his hands on his hips. "Aa-a-ah! Th' devil. It be yer own self, an' ye'll have t' make th' best o' a fair sloppy piece o' work." He grinned. "Fer one thing"—he turned his head and looked at his profile out of the corner of his eye—"Tom, yer nose there, it ain't half bad." A pine cone splashed into the water and shattered the reflection. He picked it up and flung it into the forest.

He looked about. An hour earlier he had suddenly found himself engulfed in a new world, surrounded by an unending sea of tall pine trees that formed a green canopy overhead. Their needles and cones and twisted trunks and branches made tortured, spiky shapes against the late sun. The deeply seamed bark glinted golden brown. Beneath the trees there was a low growth of blueberry bushes, and the floor of the forest was carpeted with pine needles and strange lichens, ferns and mosses. Little pine seedlings struggled upward everywhere for a share of the blue sky.

But strangest of all was the floor itself—the fine white beach sand beneath it all. And now this stream that snaked its way through the woods with its copper-colored water and softly bubbling sounds.

"Aye—it come sudden like openin' a door. Like they wuz jist bound t' try somethin' brand new."

A gust of wind sighed through the tops of the pines. Tree limbs rubbing against each other made a weird music. He shivered and stood up. A chill had begun to settle in the woods. The boy dressed. Sitting against the base of a large tree, he chewed slowly on his last chunk of bread.

"An' wot," he mused, "d' ye plan t' do now?" He licked his

lips. "She bakes like I remember me own mum did. But ye best not look t' havin' such fine victuals every day! It be a fine beginnin' but——"

He listened to the strange sounds of the forest. Animals were on the prowl, ready for the night's grim hunting. The death scream of an unlucky rabbit sent chills down his back. He had passed packs of grunting, mean-looking hogs rooting on the forest floor for the droppings of the nut trees. The sinking sun was now a bloody disk through the jagged lacework of the trees, casting long, dark shadows in the forest.

Again the sweep's thoughts wandered back down the road, over the long day, to Philadelphia. That same sun would be making the bricks glow—and it would be glancing off the bayonets and scarlet uniforms of the British soldiers. It would be a city of red all right—including Gilligan's red-faced rage at losing another boy. The other sweeps would roam the city till late tonight, staying clear of the plasterer. He pictured each of them in his mind. What fine fellows they seemed. He grinned fondly. "Aye—they wuz good lads fer all that. They wuz all I had. Wuz me an' them agin' th' rest. Me mates, they wuz."

With that thought and the last bite of bread swallowed, his mood turned black as the pines against the sun. He felt as if he had a bone stuck in his throat. "Who d' ye think ye are, leavin' yer mates like ye wuz so grand? Yer free t' run like a rabbit is all—hippity hop. Runnin' away from somethin' all th' time. Ye'll not find a welcome nowheres—'cept t' clean a flue or a cesspool or such."

Had it not been for the sudden darkness, he would have

started back to the city then and there. But instead, he crawled under the low protective branches of a pine where he fell at last into a troubled sleep.

8

MYSTERIOUS CARGO

THE BOY thrashed about and struggled to free himself from the rope, but his arms felt strange, flapping helplessly, like wings. Mr. Gilligan roared with laughter and leaned over the chimney, holding him tightly. "Th' blacker th' bird, th' cleaner th' chimney," he cried out to several grinning, scarlet-clad soldiers. "We'll teach this goose t' stay home. It's down we go an' up, an' down, an' up, an' ——"

The boy's eyes opened wildly, and it was a long, fearful moment before he remembered where he was. He lay on the sand, breathing heavily. "Ah-h! Devil take it—ye'd think at least ye could catch a wink or two in peace."

He crawled out of his nest and splashed some water on his face. A damp early morning mist hung over the stream and stretched fingers into the woods. He stepped out onto the rutted, sand road and stood indecisively for a time. Then he heard the muffled clopping of hooves, the creaking of wagon wheels and the slap and jingle of harness approaching from the east.

A horse snorted loudly and voices shouted. The sweep jumped
back into the undergrowth.

In a few minutes the sounds were almost upon him, and
then the dim shapes of the lead horses appeared in the mists.
Straining, with the shouts of the wagoners and the cracking of
rawhide whips, a team of four dragged a rocking wagon
through the deep, soft ruts on either side of the little log bridge
that crossed the stream. It was heaped with a load of salt hay.
The boy looked on puzzled. *It be fearful heavy hay t' make th'*
nags sweat so, he thought. It slowly creaked off.

A second wagon lumbered past in the same manner. It too
was loaded with hay and made heavy weather of it, its axles
groaning loudly. The condition of the road grew worse; the
ruts further churned and deepened.

The third wagon, heavily laden with firewood, bogged down
hopelessly. The horses struggled and the wagoners swore and
cracked their whips in vain. The men from the other wagons
returned to help and, cursing and sweating, they began unloading the wagon, stacking the wood on the other side of the
bridge.

The sweep had crept closer, thinking to reveal himself and
strike a bargain for some breakfast, but now he stopped and
raised his eyebrows in surprise. One of the teamsters had lifted
an armload of wood. Revealed beneath it was the unmistakable
black iron barrel of a cannon. As more of the wood was removed, more cannon appeared, as well as several wooden
casks with the smooth round tops of cannon balls showing.

Having lightened the load and by heaving on the wagon
along with the team the wagoners were able finally to free

their mysterious cargo. Throughout their labors they had nervously looked up and down the road. Now one called out. "Ye'd best git th' iron covered quick, lads. There's no tellin' what Tory mob ye'll meet on th' road—they be comin' out o' th' ground fer fair—with th' king's men nigh t' Philadelphia." He strode to the lead wagon. "We'll be takin' th' turn t' Dunks Ferry, lads."

The sweep watched from his cover until the caravan had disappeared. *Ye might have snared a biscuit or somethin' there—but mebbe got yer head split too.* He frowned. *If there be one thing I've learnt—if ye wants t' go on livin', ye don't stick yer nose inta other people's secrets.* He turned and looked down the road in the direction the wagons had come from. *It be a queer load t' bring out o' th' woods.*

He started slowly down the road, not back toward Philadelphia, but to the east. The mists had disappeared, and the sun of a new day peered hopefully through the pines. The night chill soon wore off with his exertion. "Ye'd be addled t' go back," he said aloud. "Ye be a runaway t' Gilligan now, no matter wot! An' anyway, there be things t' see on this road."

A slight, lingering trace of his bad dream flickered uncomfortably across his mind for a moment. Then, as dreams do, it drifted off like the mists.

9

IRON

THE SWEEP felt the pounding through the soles of his shoes before he heard the noise. A faint shuddering beat of the earth, as if somewhere in the woods ahead a giant blacksmith hammered at an enormous anvil. Darkness had fallen over the Pines now, but he walked on, drawn by the power of the thing that lay ahead. Soon he saw a faint orange glow rising and falling above the ragged black silhouette of the trees.

The woods thinned, and to one side he saw the shimmering reflection of a lake. Around a last curve of the road the sweep came to a halt. In the clearing before him, dominating a strange scene, stood the dark outline of a pyramid-shaped structure. From its top an orange flame pulsed with a regular rhythm— roaring with power along with the great hammer. To one side a water wheel revolved slowly. A narrow wooden trestle ran from a bank of earth across to a platform near the flaming stack of the pyramid. Dark figures pushed carts back and forth over this, dumping their loads into a seemingly bottom-less maw, feeding the squat monster.

All about were the crouching buildings of a fair-sized settlement. The feeble glow of candlelight lit a window here and there.

The sweep moved closer to the inferno and watched from the shadows of a small shed. At one side of the structure, a group of men worked at shaping a curious network of trenches in a bed of sand at its base. Presently one of the group bent to an arched opening in the stone and moments later a fiercely glowing river of red began to flow into the trenches.

The sweep stepped back further into the shadows, but the heat still washed over him and the glow reflected redly on his face. He spoke softly to the scene. "Aye—if it ain't th' end o' th' world, then it be black magic, that's wot."

He didn't know how long he had stood there, his eyes wide, his mouth open. He was startled down to his shoes when he heard the voice at his side.

"Looks fer fair like ye seen a spirit or somethin'. Or be ye th' village idiot mebbe?" A dark figure stood holding two wooden buckets, looking at the sweep. He jerked his head toward the houses of the town. "Ye'd best be gettin' back t' yer mum hadn't ye?"

The sweep looked at the figure before him and breathed a sigh of relief—he was only a boy himself. He pointed to the scene suspiciously. "Wot be this place?"

The youth tipped his head sideways and lifted an eyebrow. "It be Batsto Ironworks is wot it be." He glanced around at the fingers of orange flowing into the trenches, then back at the sweep's gaping face. "An' that be iron, ye addlehead." He grunted and lifted the heavy water-filled buckets and started off—then turned back. "An' where d'ye come from if ye don't know 'bout iron?" He looked closely at the sweep for the first time and frowned. "Yer not much t' look at, are ye? Wot be them ugly black ——"

The sweep looked about. He backed off and picked up a heavy stick. He swung it back and forth and grinned. "Them? Why they be part o' me disguise. I be really o' royal blood—an' not used t' listenin' t' lip like that from jist any bloody ol' bucket boy."

The other boy's eyes went to the stick. He laughed. "Oo-o-o! Ain't ye th' fearsome little devil? Ye makes me fair shake ye does." He dropped the buckets and his hand went to his waist. The glint of a knife appeared, and they faced each other in the shadows. "Lissen," the boy sneered, "I'll give ye some advice 'fore I slice ye." He looked at the outline of an imposing stone house, then back at the sweep with a sly grin. "If ye be runnin', if ye knows wot I means, ye'd best not tarry around here. Mr. Ball"—he waved the blade toward the stone house— "Mr. Ball may make cannon an' shot for Genr'l Washington, but when it comes t' runaways—'specially a stinkin', black, ugly one like yerself—well, he an' th' king jist might see eye t' eye on that."

The sweep stared wordlessly at the grinning face. *Th' devil, Tom,* he thought. *Yer head be stuffed from ear t' ear with soot! Ye jist comes walkin' in t' th' town like a fine gintleman an' blabs with th' first one ye sees—an' it's a lucky thing ye din' see Mr. Ball hisself first. Aye.* He flung down the stick. *All ye needs is t' start fightin' soon as ye gits here.*

"If I wuz you, I'd jist kind o' fade in t' th' woods." The boy looked at the black fringe of the pines that pressed in all about them. "There be lots o' eyes lookin' out from behind them trees." He laughed without humor. "Ye'll find yer spot out there." He waited for a moment and nodded his head. "Aye!" he sneered. He put his blade back in its sheath. He picked up the buckets and staggered off toward the men at the furnace.

The sweep followed along beside him. "Where be th' ships?" he called out above the roar of the furnace.

The boy looked down at him. "Ye'll find 'em at th' Forks— over th' bridge by th' gristmill an' then t' th' left in about a mile." He snickered. "Is th' gintleman from th' city goin' t' buy hisself a cargo?"

10

THE GAME

THE SWEEP backed slowly away from the furnace. He lingered for a time and watched the bubbling liquid harden and turn into dull brown lengths of iron.

Behind him, up at the stone house, a square of light appeared, then blinked out as a door was opened and then closed. A short time later the glow of the furnace lit the approaching form of a portly, elegantly dressed man accompanied by a more muscular fellow in plainer garb. They headed for the furnace, their path taking them close to the sweep.

"And the blast, it goes well? We can't afford many puffs like the other day. The iron is needed as never before by the army."

"As well as a body can hope, Mr. Ball—though o' course th' charge can go up in a puff at any time fer no reason we know of, even with th' latest methods."

The sweep dropped his head between his shoulders and started to walk past them toward the town.

"Yes—well, I'm sure you understand the urgency." The

cultivated voice paused. "Hello? Whose ragged little lad is this? I have not seen you here before."

The sweep bowed—touched his forehead with a finger. "Good evenin', Mr. Ball, sir." He strode boldly past, hearing that gentleman say, "I must be getting forgetful. He's a respectful little chap, but I see that his family dresses him in a manner that befits Batsto."

The boy broke into a run as soon as he rounded the first building, and he didn't slow to a walk until he had passed through the town, had crossed the small bridge below the creaking mill, and was well along the road to the Forks.

The beating of the hammer faded behind him, and he became aware of new sounds ahead floating faintly on the breeze. They grew into a mingling of shouts and laughter, scraping fiddles and singing as he entered the little village of the Forks. There was revelry in the air and, the sweep sniffed, there were the smells of sailing ships too—like Water Street in Philadelphia. And there were the masts and the rigging rising against the moon—and the river, lit by the path of its bright reflection, its banks overhung by a tangle of pines and cedars, twisting mysteriously off into the darkness toward the sea. He gazed at the sloops and schooners riding silently on the black waters at the crude piers.

This was the place, the hideaway where the rebel privateers brought their captured prizes—here on this point of swampy land where the Mullica split into its branches. They were protected from the British fleet by the shoal waters and the shifting treachery of the sand bars at the ocean inlet, and by the length of this sinuous river.

The sweep paused before a substantial clapboard house. A sign, proclaiming it to be Wescoat's Tavern, creaked faintly in the breeze. A smartly dressed gentleman, bursts of lace showing at the neck and cuffs of his plum-colored coat, stepped up to the door and, as it opened briefly, it revealed a glimpse of a smoky roomful of similarly well dressed men. The figures moved vaguely behind the steamy windows.

The boy walked on toward a group of rough log buildings—the source of the evening's raucous noises. He looked into one, through a thick fog of tobacco smoke. A skinny negro scratched on a fiddle, and a tangle of shadowy figures danced madly on the dirt floor. A fat, sweating man in one corner, behind a fence of wooden bars, and a scurrying serving boy dispensed refreshments from casks and bottles.

The sweep sidled into the room and, after some time, managed to get the attention of the serving boy by holding up a coin. With a surly nod he disappeared toward the rear of the building and returned with a greasy wooden trencher laden with a cold joint of pork and a chunk of corn bread. The sweep crouched in a corner and bit ravenously into the meat.

He was tired after the long day, but the food revived him. His eyes glittered with excitement. It was good to be with people again. The carousing and the noise was reassuring and familiar. Sailors and swamp men, ironworkers and cutthroats of every style ebbed and flowed in the dim light cast by a few sputtering candles in sconces on the walls. Two fights had already erupted. The fists and bottles flew. The proprietor had slammed down the hinged overhead section of bars, completely enclosing him and his precious stores, until the storm had passed. The sweep could almost believe that he was back in Philadelphia, that he would soon be singing and shouting his way back to Gilligan's with the other sweeps.

He got to his feet and made his way about the edge of the room until he came to a group surrounding a rough table where a game of checkers was underway. He grinned. *Ah-h, Tom! They do be playin' th' game ye favors most.* There was money on the table. The sweep felt for the coins left in his pouch and watched intently.

When a sailor had finished a game and stamped off, cursing in disgust, the sweep quickly slid onto his stool and faced the man across the board. "I'll play ye."

His opponent was smooth-shaven, though he might well have used a beard, for an ugly scar creased his cheek from ear to chin. His close-set eyes darted about restlessly from their deep sockets. Now they studied the boy, who was grateful for the shadows that hid his face. The man looked up at his companions, and something approaching a smile flickered briefly.

"This is a pretty joke." He pushed away from the table.

"Mebbe 'e be a powder monkey from the ships," grunted one of them.

The sweep flung some coins on the table and challenged the man boldly. "Ye be an easy mark, I sez."

The man rose nicely to the bait. "Hah! A rude tongue here! Bold as brass he is!" He hitched up to the table. "Best we teach the impudent mite a lesson."

An hour later the man sat hunched at the edge of his stool,

head cradled in his hands, biting his lip, studying the board. The crowd stood silently watching. The dim yellow light glinted dully on a small pile of coins in front of the sweep. The man's hand hung doubtfully over a piece, then made the move. The boy reached out quickly for the win, and swept another battered coin to his pile. He stood up and filled his pouch and distributed the rest heavily in his pockets. "I be thankin' ye, sir, fer th' games." His eyes took in the rough crowd towering about him. "I'd best be leavin'." He turned to go, and the light fell clearly across his face.

The quiet was broken. "It be a sweep—fer certain it be!" A

big hand grabbed him. "An' that do explain it, captain—a thievin', cheatin' soot devil from th' city." Voices rose. "Shake th' coin loose o' him, I sez. No sweet babe here!"

The sweep's opponent had been leaning forward, palms on the table, studying the boy. "Let him go!" It was said quietly, but the hand fell from the sweep's arm.

The boy looked about briefly through the haze of smoke

and then quickly left the tavern. He didn't notice the men who slipped out of the door just ahead of him. He drifted along the front of the tavern and slapped at his pockets. "Ye jingle an' jangle like church bells, Tom. Aye—yer a gintleman o' means! It do be passin' strange how a body's fortunes kin change an' —"

He saw a slight movement in the blackness around the corner of the tavern, and he spun about to run. But powerful hands reached out and grabbed him by his jacket and lifted him off the ground like a cat lifted by the scruff of its neck. He struggled furiously—legs churning the air—as his cursing assailants pulled him into the shadows and quickly rifled his pockets and grabbed the pouch. "Quick, in t' th' river with th' bloody wildcat." The sweep ducked his head down and sank his teeth with all his might into the arm that encircled his chest. The hoarse whisper became a terrible bellow of pain. The sweep was flung to the ground.

Footsteps followed the blindly running boy for a time and then stopped. "Ye black runaway soot devil! Ye damned puny scum! Don't ye stop yer runnin' cuz we be after ye! Ye hear?"

The sweep stood in the deep shadows of a cedar and panted heavily. He spat into the darkness and wiped his mouth. "Devil take it, but I put me mark on somebody fer fair!" He laughed softly. "Wuz a tough, hairy ole joint o' meat it wuz!"

11

ALONE

TWO DAYS after having fled the Forks, the boy looked gloomily at his prospects—especially after what had happened a few minutes past, back by the ore scows.

His breathing and the rapid beat of his heart had finally returned to normal. He lifted his face from its cool pillow of moss, raised himself on his elbows and listened attentively. The receding voices could barely be heard now. He had flung himself down, exhausted, on a tangled network of stringy roots and moss that formed a spongy floor in this part of the swamp. Now, as he moved, it sagged uncertainly under him. He knew what lay beneath. He had gone into the reddish, sucking slime to his waist before he'd grabbed a branch and pulled himself clear. He wriggled his toes and frowned. Somewhere in the depths of the muck he had parted company with his shoes. He pulled his muddy coat close around his neck.

After a time his dark eyes no longer darted about. They came to rest, unseeing, on the deeply creased bark of a cedar. He cupped his chin in his hands.

"Ah-h—me fine adventure." His mouth made a grim smile. "It looked better from Gilligan's than it do from here. Brung yer troubles right along with ye." A frown erased the smile in the changing play of mood on his face. "An' now ye've been shot at fer a change! Like a bloody rabbit." He had heard the half-inch lead ball sing past his ear and had seen it rip into a tree ahead of him, scattering bark and tearing up the fleshy wood beneath like an invisible iron fist. "All fer takin' jist a little piece o' bread." Remembering, he searched around inside his shirt and withdrew a somewhat soggy chunk of bread wrapped around a bit of cheese. He ate slowly. "Be it really stealin' t' take wot ye needs t' live?"

Of course, he thought, it had been a mistake to return again to the same place—to where the men were digging up the reddish stuff at the edge of the swamp, by the narrow river. They loaded it into long narrow scows and floated them downstream, toward Batsto. It was a mystery to him what they were doing, but he had seen them return to a small scow tied to some trees at mealtime, and he had paid it several highly successful visits himself before this last one, when he had been met by an armed welcoming committee. He'd been chased back here, deeper into the swamp than he had been before.

He had found that, like a rabbit, he had certain advantages in the chase. He was a small, quick target, and he was light enough to flit over the roots and logs that sank into the ooze under the weight of a grown man. And he had the terror of a scared rabbit too, which gave his frail body extra strength and endurance. But he found small comfort in this.

He finished eating and got to his feet. "Yer livin' like a

blasted beastie—but yer sure not much good at it." He rubbed his thin arms but his teeth still chattered uncontrollably. "T' be a proper beastie, yer supposed t' have a fine fur coat fer one thing, an' claws an' big teeth, an' eyes wot kin see in th' dark— an' yer friends an' family crawlin' around t' keep ye company." He looked about at the dismal swamp. The light of day filtered down dimly through the tight umbrella of cedar branches overhead. A cawing bird whirred by, and strange splashings and rustlings sounded all about as the busy life went on.

The sweep peered about uncertainly for a few moments, then set off resolutely through the swamp, hopping from root to root, splashing occasionally into dark pools of stagnant water, pausing and looking about—a small figure growing smaller until the tangled growth had swallowed him up.

A squirrel ran along a fallen tree and in a graceful leap, landed on the mossy tangle where the boy had rested. He raised himself on his hind legs, looked this way and that, gobbled up a crumb of bread which lay there, white against the dark moss, and in another surefooted leap disappeared as quickly as he had arrived.

12

THE CHARCOAL BURNER

THE CHARCOAL BURNER was limping more than usual. It was the wet weather that always did it—and the damp, raw northeaster had been moaning through the pines for two days now. After all the years it seemed as if the piece of shot from the French brig was tearing through his leg with every step. A steady stream of profanity, addressed to the entire French nation, followed in his wake.

He doggedly went about his task, circling slowly around what appeared to be a smoking dome of earth, about 25 feet in diameter and perhaps eight feet high. Occasionally he would poke a long pole into the pile, observe the wind-blown smoke for a time and then repeat the process further on. His face and hands were sooty, and the sandy clearing was darkened with bits and pieces of charcoal. All about was a wasteland of tree stumps through which a narrow stream, swollen from the rain, flowed swiftly. A rude log hut stood nearby, and over the coals of a small fire hung a small iron pot.

After a time he paused, hands on hips, and peered about impatiently, looking for someone who was clearly past due. A dense growth of beard and heavy brows bunched angrily, and his red eyes glared out from behind it all like an injured animal peering from a tangle of underbrush. Cursing and muttering, he limped around the smoldering mound toward the hut. He lurched past the simmering pot, into the shelter and rummaged about noisily. He stepped outside with a brown earthenware jug. Hoisting it level with his ear he shook it, and then exploded into a new frenzy of profanity. Tilting his head far back, he upended the jug and drained the few drops that remained. Wiping his ragged beard with the back of his hand, he angrily flung the jug far into the field where it shattered in pieces against a stump. The effort wrenched painfully at his back. His eye fell on the iron pot, and he kicked at it viciously with his good leg, sending it and its contents flying. Roaring in rage, he brushed off the hot splatterings of the stew where it had landed on him. Far gone now in his fury, he spun about, looking for a new victim—and he saw one approaching the hut. He blinked redly, looked at the figure for a moment, then reached into the hut and pulled out an old, pitted and rusty cutlass. He slashed it through the air several times with the look of one who was used to the weapon and snorted with satisfaction.

The tall, gangling, slack-jointed fellow crossed the clearing unsteadily, a silly grin on his face and a jug swinging loosely from a hooked finger. He turned the corner of the hut and swayed to an abrupt halt. The end of the cutlass pointed at his belly nicked lightly at his shirt. He backed off a step and licked his lips nervously. His bleary eyes focused with difficulty.

The charcoal burner matched his step and swung the blade up to his bobbing Adam's apple. "Ah, Ben, me loyal helper," he breathed heavily, smiling a ghastly smile, "How wuz all th' lads down t' Sooy's? Ye'll be wantin', no doubt, t' have a little snooze now, eh wot, me hearty? After all yer good times ye'll be needin' some rest, eh? Three days o' drinkin' th' strong waters do take it out o' a man don't it. An' havin' t' lug back that jug fer me was hard dooty too—jist set it down, Ben, that's th' good lad—an' I'll wager ye lightened it a bit on th' way."

He waggled the cutlass. "Well, 'tis jist good fun, eh wot? That thing there"—he jerked his head toward the smoking pile—"it don't matter, do it? It only be"—his voice dripped sarcasm—"it only be 50 cord o' wood, jist two weeks o' work day an' night watchin' it so it don't go t' ash. An' Mr. Ball, he don't care if he don't git his charcoal fer th' furnace, do he?" He moved forward, face flushed. Ben, his bloodshot eyes now riveted to the waving tip of the cutlass, stumbled slowly backward before him. "An' anyway"—the voice rose to a cracked shout—"ol' Black John don't mind stayin' up three days runnin', takin' yer watches—no shut-eye, no rest, nor a drop o' spirits left t' ease the blasted leg!"

In spite of the leg he began to move faster, coattail flapping in the wind and drizzle, slashing at Ben's dancing ankles until the poor fellow suddenly turned and took to his heels. "An' with th' blasted wind th' stack's ready t' go up like a powder

ship! Ye worthless lout! Git back t' Sooy's an' yer friends an'
don't come back or, mark me well, I'll run iron through yer
black heart fer fair." He continued limping furiously after
Ben, waving his cutlass against the stormy sky, hurling in-
vectives at his fleeing back until his voice faded into the sound
of the wind in the trees.

A strange calm descended over the charcoal pit. The sweep
lifted his head cautiously from behind a stump and looked
after them. "Blast. A body could starve t' death waitin' fer th'
ol' beard t' leave th' pile! Th' smell o' that pot's been near t'
killin' me." He flung himself toward the hut. He was even
thinner than when he had run from the ore raisers. His clothes
were tattered, his hair hung lank about his face.

He fell upon the scraps of meat scattered about on the

ground by the fire like a vulture, stuffing them into his mouth sand and all, his eyes darting about looking for more. He squatted down over the still warm pot and wiped it clean with his fingers. Casting it aside, he scuttled into the hut. He grabbed a filthy deerskin robe, poked about, picked up a slab of johnnycake and turned to go—and found himself facing the tip of the old beard's cutlass.

The boy dropped his load and ducked this way and that, but there was no way to slip past the blade, which followed his every move. He stood at last, trapped, sullenly staring at the dirt floor.

"So!" The burner panted from his exertion. He studied the sweep ferociously, and slowly his rasping breathing quieted. His voice grated between his teeth. "Ye knows, does ye, that th' bullet an' th' blade be th' law here? We jist takes care o' things quick"—he swished the cutlass back and forth—"an' ship-shape like."

The sweep stole a furtive look at the weapon and nervously wiped at the smears of food around his mouth. Devil be damned! His heart thudded against his ribs. He could almost feel the rusty blade scrape between them. *Ah-h! Wuz this ugly, mean ol' buzzard t' be th' last thing he'd see in his whole bloody life?* His thoughts skipped about strangely. *Wouldn't there be no soft bed, no sweet mum holdin' his hand, pattin' his hot forehead, cryin' soft like as he slowly slipped outa th' world on a downy cloud? Wouldn't there be no ——*

The gravelly old voice yanked him back. "Oughta stick ye like a porkypine. Be a good deed, it would, t' rid th' woods o' yer thievin'!" But the cutlass dropped slowly to his side. "Ah-h," he muttered, "yer a mean enough lookin' little bag o' bones. Ain't even got stewin' meat on ye." He sighed gustily, and his eyes narrowed. "Ye be a runaway—a sweep?"

The boy nodded slightly, and he felt a flicker of hope. He could almost hear the greasy old graybeard thinking—could see his eyes appraise him.

"Mebbe I be soft in th' head t' even think o' it. A sweep! A thievin' soot devil!" He glanced at the smoking mound, then at the boy.

"Lookee here, we both got bad troubles. On a lee shore we be, fer certain. Ye're near starvin' from th' looks o' it, an' I be needin' a helper or I'll drop in me tracks." He scratched vigorously at something crawling in his beard and made a noise that might have been a laugh. "Ye can't be no worse 'n th' last, an' Ol' John don't never aim t' see th' pearly gates hisself." He fixed his best eye, burning like a hot coal, on the sweep. "Ye gits victuals an' a roof—an' ye helps me with th' stack. An' no questions asked. Wot say?"

The sweep grinned slightly at the sooty face before him. *A-a-h, Tom,* he thought, *ye comes like an arrow, all this way, t' th' soot—it be yer' bloomin' fate.*

"Quit yer silly grinnin' an' gimme an answer—or I'll be changin' me mind an'——"

The sweep nodded. "I'll help ye."

But his reply was barely out of his mouth when the sullenly smoldering stack behind them erupted with a dull explosion that filled the air with hurtling, flaming bits and chunks of wood and red-hot coals and earth. Smoke and dust billowed about madly in the wind and mist.

As the swirling debris settled back to earth, the boy and the man gaped silently at the destruction. Then the wild-eyed charcoal burner, slashing his cutlass about, stamping and cursing and shrieking to the heavens, exploded in a mad dance of wrath that held the boy transfixed.

13

A NEW HOME

THE last of the wood haulers had left, the last taunt had been flung at the charcoal burner, and the crude ox-drawn sledges had bumped off across the treeless barren toward the receding line of the pines where the axmen worked. Fifty cords of wood—cut in four-foot lengths, split into billets—and great piles of smaller branches of lapwood lay stacked in a circle about the charcoal pit.

The charcoal burner had been subdued and withdrawn all through the labor of cleaning up the pit and unloading the wood. Hat in hand he had listened to the angry man who came out from Batsto. He had refreshed himself often from the jug. He had scarcely spoken a word to the sweep since the stack had blown, communicating in grunts and nods and waves of the hand.

The sweep had done as he was told, had eaten hungrily of the rough fare and had slept gratefully beneath a vermin-infested robe in the hut, for the mid-October nights were chill.

He had patched up his clothes somewhat with the charcoal burner's needle and odd bits of cloth.

Now the charcoal burner surveyed the wood dourly. He turned to the sweep and spat in the sand. "So we be tryin' again, Soot Devil."

First they placed a pole, about 18 feet long, upright in the center of what was called the pit, a flat circle about 30 feet in diameter. Around the pole they built a triangular lattice of the small lapwood. "It be th' chimbly," grunted the charcoal burner. All about this they stacked the four-foot billets on end, slowly working out toward the edge of the pit where the billets slanted inward. Then the charcoal burner clambered up on the solidly stacked base, and the sweep passed more billets up to him. These were carefully placed as the bottom ones had been, any empty spaces being filled in with the small lapwood. By the last light of the evening they climbed a ladder and spread a layer of lapwood on top of this, which rounded off the pile into a domelike shape.

Exhausted, they plodded to the hut. Lighting a pine splint in the embers of the fire, they squatted on the ground, and by its light they speared chunks of meat out of the pot with knives, and munched johnnycake. They each took turns at the jug. Only the sounds of chewing and swallowing, their weary breathing, the scrape of a knife against the pot broke the stillness.

Later they lay on the sand floor of the darkened hut in the last brief moments of wakefulness. The charcoal burner's muffled sarcasm sounded through beard and robe. "Like yer new trade, Soot Devil?"

"Better'n climbin' flues," muttered the sweep. He dropped off into the dreamless sleep of utter exhaustion.

With the first light of the morning they returned to their work on the stack. Through the long day they spread a thick layer of leaves over the dome, and then a deep layer of sooty sand on top of them. Late in the afternoon they filled the stick chimney with small kindling. The charcoal burner straightened up slowly. "Done," he breathed. "It be ready fer burnin'."

The days of work had taken their toll. Cursing through whitened lips, he limped painfully to the hut and sat heavily on a log before the fire. He took a long pull on the jug and stared balefully at the mountain of wood, then at the sweep who had built up the fire and now brought food out of the hut.

"So there it be again," he barked belligerently. "Jist where it wuz three weeks back." He rubbed his outstretched leg and cursed. "Tell me, Soot Devil, wot th' meanin' be—all th' work, th' waste, jist gone. An' then pretty soon me an' you too, th' same way, jist gone an' no sign we wuz ever here?" He eyed the sweep, who stared wordlessly into the coals. "Ah-h—yer not thinkin' them thoughts yet, sweep?" He laughed harshly. "Soon enough, soon enough ye will!"

The sweep placed the simmering pot between them and began to eat. He gnawed on a tough piece of rabbit, swallowed, and stabbed his knife into the pot for another. "Me name be Tom Fry," he said as he put it into his mouth.

The charcoal burner looked sideways at the boy. "So? Tom Fry, eh wot? An' I be King George," he chuckled grimly. "But they jist calls me Ol' John. Ain't we a purty pair—ain't we jist

a couple o' wonders o' th' bloomin' world! Th' bloody beginnin'
an' th' end ye might say!"

They fell silent again. It was nearly dark when they finished
eating. The charcoal burner got slowly to his feet and waved
toward a shovel. "Git a load o' coals from th' fire an' we'll start
th' pile up."

They climbed the ladder to the top of the stack, carefully
passing up the coals. The charcoal burner dumped the glowing load down the chimney, and then sealed the top with sticks
and leaves and sand.

Seated before the fire once more they watched the narrow
band of red disappear in the western sky. After a time the
charcoal burner waved a hand at the stack. "D' ye know wot
we be doin' there?"

The sweep chuckled into the darkness. "Tryin' t' make charcoal is wot I'd say."

The man glared at the boy. "An' ain't ye still th' saucy soot
devil though—laughin' at me now, makin' yer little jokes!" His
voice rose. "An' where has yer jokes got ye so far? Half-starved
is where they've got ye! Me name," he mimicked the sweep's
words, "me name be Tom Fry. Ain't that somethin'!" He
picked up the jug.

The sweep stood up. He heaved a stick of wood out among
the stumps. "An' if ye don't laugh wot? Ye laugh—or ye drown
in yer tears." He raked his fingers through his hair. "Ye asks
wot th' meanin' be—have I been thinkin' an' all! Aye—I been
thinkin.' Been thinkin' about wot sweet god sticks his finger at
me an' makes me a bloody soot devil—somethin' wot's spat on

like a bloomin' pig! That be wot I been thinkin'!" He stared into the woods and clenched his teeth.

When he looked back at the fire, the charcoal burner was lost in his own thoughts, far away. "Aye," the sweep muttered, "mebbe it ain't enough, th' laughin'." The bearded charcoal burner stared down at the sand, rocking slightly, rubbing his leg and cursing softly. The boy turned and went into the hut.

Wrapped in his robe he watched the figure at the fire. The jug was lifted at regular intervals.

"Ah-h. There be a mad one. Is that th' way ye'll be—askin' them questions, bristly as a porkypine, crazy mad at a little joke like that?" He lay on his back and tried to see ahead— to see himself limping, bearded, bitter and old. Firelight glittered on the old cutlass, hanging from a peg. "Wot's th' ol' beard been doin' all th' years wot's soured him so?" The boy pulled the robe tightly around his shoulders. "Well—yer in here, under some skins an' eatin' instead o' prowlin' out there in th' woods like a beastie. Give th' beard his marks fer that." But he shivered in spite of the robe.

14

THE STACK

THE POLE jabbed persistently in the boy's ribs until, growling and pawing at the bothersome thing, he awoke and heaved out from under the skins. The morning sun was above the jagged tops of the pines.

"Wot d' ye think I be—a bloomin' pincushion?"

The charcoal burner pulled his long pole back out of the hut and lifted a tangled eyebrow.

"An' it must be very fancy, how ye lives in th' city, fer sure. Ye be used t' dainty food an' wines an' fine sheets t' sleep on an' all, no doubt." He squinted at the sun, then looked to the stack from which wisps of smoke wafted.

"I beg ye a thousan' pardons fer interruptin' yer sweet dreams"—he bowed low—"but I wuz thinkin' that since yer lordship do enjoy me roof an' victuals so, ye wouldn't mind givin' jist a little o' yer expert help an' advice—when ye feels up t' it, o' course." He rolled the good eye at the boy and swept his arm around to indicate the smoking mound behind him.

"Aa-a-a-h!" The sweep stood up and sleepily shrugged into his coat with ill humor.

The bearded man looked off to the trees and pointed carelessly to a skillet at the fire. "There be somethin'. Ye might as well eat it, I reckon."

The sweep watched him limp away. He looked at the skillet, set just so to keep a fresh-made round of johnnycake warm. He squatted by the fire and scooped up a piece with his knife. Chewing slowly, he stared into the skillet with puzzlement. "Not a bite out o' it." His eyes narrowed. "An' he let me sleep half th' mornin'." He looked suspiciously at the man over by the stack. "Wot d' ye s'pose th' old' buzzard be up to?" He finished eating and joined him warily at the pile.

The sweep was gruffly instructed in the mysteries of charcoal making. "Th' idee be t' burn it slow, so it don't jist turn t' ash. Ain't jist a big bloody campfire ye know. Ye never do burn it up—if yer lucky." He showed with his long pole how to poke vent holes into the side of the mound that faced away from the wind. If the wind changed, the holes had to be closed and new ones made. If the stack got too much air, it would just burn up. "An if th' stack don't git enough air, then th' gases collect an' "—a black cloud settled over the burner's face as he recalled the recent disaster—"well, ye saw fer yourself wot happens." The stack had to be nursed along, day and night, as if it had a sickness. They puttered around it all day, poking it and prodding it and pampering it like a great queen bee.

That evening at sunset, to the amazement of the sweep, the charcoal burner climbed up on top of the mound and com-

menced to jump up and down and stamp all over it like a mad-
man. Etched against the red sun, it looked like some savage
ritual. He shouted that he was looking for mulls—soft spots
that could burn through during the night. The cavities would
have to be filled or the pile could burn up in the night.

The sweep eyed the strange dance. "An' wot happens if ye
jumps too hard an' yer bloody soft spot caves in under ye?"

Old John continued his lame, lopsided jumping. "Aye, Tom,"
he panted, "then th' fat would be in th' fire fer fair wouldn't it?"
He cackled loudly. "Aye, Tom—it do be a grand, fine trade!"

That first night of the burning, the sweep relieved the charcoal burner at the stack in the early morning. The breeze was

steady and gentle and the moon was a bright, friendly lantern
in the sky. Smoke curled lazily from the vent holes, as it did
when it was burning properly. He sat near the stack, wrapped
in a robe, his mind wandering about, thinking the thoughts
that one has at such times. He thought of the past—of how
strange it was that he was here. He thought of all the places in
the world where he might be. Of the strange string of events
that led him, Tom Fry, across oceans, up chimneys, into
swamps, to this, of all places. And it all had just happened to
him. Or had it? "Ye wanted th' bloomin' candy din't ye?" He
grinned. "Wuz it yer blasted sweet tooth wot done it all?"

He snuggled down further in the robe and let his head rest

on a log, peering up at the stars. He thought of the people he'd known—his mother and sister, dim in the mists. Where were they? He tried again to put a picture of a father next to his mother, but still couldn't. Dead? Runaway? He lingered for a time, then rocked his head and moved on quickly to the ship, to Philadelphia, the sweeps—Gilligan. Then the face of a flaxen-haired girl swam impossibly into his thoughts. The stars glittered silently. Each person, each place had been his world for a time and then had disappeared, dropped back, became a memory in his mind. He looked about the deeply shadowed charcoal pit, heard the muffled snores from the hut. A snug berth—but this would go too. Gilligan's and the chimneys were fading already. "Aye, ye thinks yer set somewheres, but ye always jist seems t' be on yer way."

His eyelids began to grow heavy. Was Gilligan's really done with? He shut his eyes. Would he be in the Pines long—like th' —— His head nodded and jerked up once. Then slowly, slowly it rolled forward on his chest.

The moon traced its majestic path across the sky, casting its changing shadows on the charcoal pit. It took a last reproachful look through the tracery of the pines and dropped below the western horizon just as the faint light of dawn appeared in the east. The tops of the trees rustled slightly in the first gust of a new breeze. Leaves on the ground trembled, then lifted and fluttered across the clearing.

It was blowing briskly when the boy's head snapped up. Blinking, he stared about for a moment before exploding out of the robe. He threw himself toward the stack and frantically started to close the vents. He trembled with fear for the great pile. Was it his imagination or was the thing bubbling and rumbling deep within? He ranted at himself. "Aaa-h! Be ye nuthin' but a silly soot devil? Nuthin' but a blasted brush? Ah-h, ye'll muck it up fer sure ye will!" Nearly in tears and panting he raced around to the other side of the mound and started opening new vents.

He was nearly done, and the stack still stood intact in its silent, smoking dignity, when the charcoal burner appeared, yawning and scratching sleepily. He watched the boy for some minutes and nodded approvingly. "Aye, ye've got t' watch her every minute." He picked up a pole and helped the sweep. "Ye must be ready fer a snooze 'bout now." It sounded friendly.

The boy stared guiltily at the sand.

"Heard some talkin' an' yellin'—wuz that you?"

The boy nodded.

"Thought so. I does th' same—ye has t' talk." He eyed the sweep again and pulled at his beard. "I talks t' th' stack a lot— like it wuz somebody—an' t' th' animals. Ye know?"

The boy flicked a quick look at him and edged on around the pile, studying the smoke now curling from the new vents. "Ye does?" he muttered.

They worked silently until the stack seemed to be adjusted to the new wind. They leaned on their poles observing it.

"Jug's empty." The charcoal burner looked down and swept a shoe back and forth in the sand, making a smooth arc. Then, as if he had made up his mind to something, he looked at the boy. "Ye knows Sooy's? Th' tavern?"

The sweep nodded. Ha! He'd sampled their victuals. Th'

bloomin' kitchen door was open an' when th' cook stepped out, why he'd jist grabbed himself some food.

"Well I wuz thinkin'. Could ye jist run down there an' back, while I takes care o' th' stack?" He looked narrowly at the sweep from beneath his brows. His eyes went to the boy's bare feet. "An' while yer there ye kin git some shoes. Nuthin' fancy. There be a peddler or cat whipper there most times."

The picture of the charcoal burner and his former helper, Ben, came back to the boy. He smiled. "Aye. I kin do that. An' I needs foot leather fer sure."

15

BEN MAKES HIS MARK

LATER that day the sweep leaned against the slatted bar in a corner of Nicholas Sooy's rough-and-ready tavern and waited for the jug to be filled. Curiously he watched the scene before him.

A bony-faced figure in the uniform of a lieutenant in the Continental Army stood at a table. His eyes roved over the noisy crowd. In his hands he held a large sheet of paper from which he had been reading. He compressed his lips and frowned with resignation. Behind him stood several other men, more or less in the uniform of the Continental Army. Now he turned to the proprietor behind the bar.

"If ye'll be so kind sir, to serve another round"—he waved at the room—"to all these brave men." There was a hoarse cheer from the motley crowd. The ironworkers, sailors, woodcutters, and the other woods dwellers had trudged down the sandy trails to this crossroads in the wilderness to indulge in their favorite recreation.

The lieutenant coughed, cleared his throat loudly and resumed his reading.

"And the encouragement to enlist is truly liberal and generous ———"

His voice was drowned out by several loud guffaws.

". . . an annual and fully sufficient supply of good and handsome clothing, a daily allowance of a large and ample ration of provisions, together with $60 a year in gold and silver money and ———"

While the lieutenant waited for the burst of derisive laughter to die down, he scanned the faces. At length he focused his attention on a lanky, swaying figure in the front of the crowd. It was Ben, the charcoal burner's erstwhile helper. At a slight nod one of the men behind the lieutenant went to him, filled his mug once more, and put a friendly hand on his stooped shoulders. The reading resumed.

". . . this opportunity of spending a few happy years in viewing the different parts of this beautiful continent, in the honorable and truly respectable character of a soldier ———"

The lieutenant lifted an eyebrow at the titter that ran through the room.

". . . after which, he may, if he pleases, return home to his friends, with his pockets full of money and his head covered with laurels. God saved the United States."

He hurriedly rolled up the sheet and placed it on the table before him.

The rear of the room erupted again. "Yer head covered with wot, lootenant?"

"Devil take it, lootenant—did ye write that yerself? It be real poetic!"

A bedlam of laughter and shouting continued for some time. Meanwhile, Ben's eyes were becoming glassy. His mug was filled again.

The lieutenant leaned forward and placed his hands on the table. "General Washington," he cried out, "sent us especially to the beautiful Pines o' Jersey. He knows that you brave and loyal patriots will not fail your commander in chief. The British are in Philadelphia—uh, trapped by our powerful forces. With a few more fine soldiers we shall drive them into the sea!" He paused dramatically. "And now—will the brave volunteers step forward, line up in orderly fashion so Corporal Pickering here can help ye fill out the papers."

A heavy silence fell over the room. The lieutenant's fingers drummed impatiently on the table. Finally his eyes returned to Ben. A slow smile creased his face. The soldier who was now supporting Ben, and whispering in his ear, drew him forward to the table and sat him heavily in a chair by Corporal Pickering.

"Ah. There we are. The first brave man to step forward." He strode up and down clapping his hands. "Come, m' lads, step up now. The ice is broken." He paused, leaned over Ben's sagging shoulder and watched as the corporal placed a quill pen in his fingers. He reached out and steered Ben's hand as he made his mark. "There. And a fine soldier ye'll be!"

The sweep paid for the jug and stood for a time by the door.

The lieutenant faced the crowd again and pointed to a burly

young fellow. "You there. How about it, me lad—for glory and for country?"

"Me? Why, lootenant, I favors it, I really does, but ye see, I be workin' down t' Batsto makin' cannon balls fer ye. The Congress has given us fellers an—ah—an exemption—that be th' word mates? Ye might say they jist plain ordered us t' stay here." He smiled broadly. "Some o' us unlucky ones got t' stay home an' support th' brave soljers." A ragged cheer went up. He grinned over at Ben, whose head now rested peacefully on the table.

The lieutenant pointed to another broad-shouldered youth. "And you?"

"Well," he said, winking at the men at his table, "ye see, I be signed aboard a privateerin' ship jist last night. Th' *Rattlesnake,* down t' Chestnut Neck. We be off t' fight th' British too an' ——"

"An' at a heap better pay too, wot say Adam?" said a sarcastic voice.

"And you? Come lads!"

"Ye see lootenant, we do admire th' brave soljers—but me old lady ——"

No further recruits were enlisted at Sooy's that day.

The sweep stepped outside with his jug and watched the small party of soldiers hoist poor Ben aboard a broken-down nag and set off down the sandy road toward the Delaware. A soldier on another horse rode beside him, holding him upright in the saddle.

16

━━━◆◆●━━━

THE CAT WHIPPER

INSIDE the tavern the sounds of hilarity rose to a new pitch. The sweep walked back to the small shed behind the main house and watched the little weather-beaten kernel of a man stitch up his shoes. Cat Whipper they called him. He managed to keep busy, traveling about, making simple shoes for the people in the Pines. He carried a few wooden lasts to build the shoes around. With them he could sort of fit almost anybody's foot—give or take an inch or two. He sat on his bench, which traveled with him on a wheelbarrow, and held the shoe between his knees, whipping the cat, sewing the sole to the uppers with hog-bristle needles. He looked up at the sweep with a speculative eye.

"Steppin' up in th' world I'd say."

The sweep watched the gnarled, practiced hands, the needle and thread. He looked over at a mule-drawn wagon getting underway after a stop at the tavern. It was laden with casks from a saltworks on the coast. The teamsters had enjoyed their visit, and the crisp air rang with the cracking of their whips. He looked back at the shoe.

"When yer at th' bottom, it be th' only way t' go."

"Aye. Well I could make a guess on ye, but th' bite o' yer money is good. I don't much care where it or yerself comes from." He held the half-finished shoe up and studied it. "It'll be a mite big fer ye, but ye kin stuff it with rags," he said, "till ye grows up to it." He put it between his knees again. He nodded toward the tavern.

"So ye din't enlist?"

The sweep spat in the sand. "Th' fightin' be no business o' mine."

"Aye. Well it do seem t' be a good business fer some people." He nodded toward the wagon as it creaked off. "That salt there, fer instance. Two shillings a bushel at th' shore, an' they sells it fer seven pounds t' th' bleedin' army." He paused in his work and chuckled. "Aye. There be ways t' make bein' a patriot pay! Like them fine gintlemen ye sees at Batsto an' th' Forks. Got th' world by th' thumbs they do. It be their public dooty t' make cannon balls—an' money—an' t' buy an' sell the cargoes wot th' privateerin' ships ketch. Not that it ain't danger-ous work, me boy. Sometimes they gits bit terrible bad by th' flies." He chuckled and placed the wooden pegs used to fasten the heels between his lips and reluctantly fell silent.

The boy got up and stepped out into the sunlit yard. He leaned against the fence that in summer enclosed the tavern's vegetable garden. Several scrawny, molting chickens wandered about, and he absently watched their aimless peckings. "Ah—he be a talky one fer sure."

The muffled sounds from the tavern rose and fell in the background. All day long the steady trickle of comings and goings had continued. With each opening of the barroom door a raucous burst of noise would escape—to be cut off as the door slammed shut. It was during such an eruption, as he stood watching the chickens, that a horse and rider clopped softly into the yard behind the sweep. The man dismounted, fastened the reins to the fence and started for the tavern. His glance fell on the boy and he paused.

"Ah-h! My worthy opponent, I believe!"

The sweep spun around and looked up at the tall man. A tricorn hat shaded the smooth, thinly smiling face with the deepset eyes and the long scar that disfigured one side. The sweep's eyes darted about, saw that the man was alone and returned more calmly to the figure before him.

"I trust ye put your winnings to good use—didn't fritter away the earnings of such a rare talent in places like this?"

The sweep scowled. "Ye might know yerself wot happened t' m' winnin's bettern' me, comes t' that."

The man cocked his head at the boy. "Devil take it—isn't he still the impudent sweep. I would think that one who has come to us directly from Philadelphia, that great seat of civilization—the very Athens of America, they say—I would think that he would temper the raw edges of his great talent with a dash of humility. And perhaps a pinch of civility, too." He bowed low. "Good day to you, young sir." He turned and strode off toward the tavern door.

The sweep watched him disappear into the building. He moved thoughtfully back into the shed.

The cat whipper glanced curiously at him. "Ye knows th' captain does ye?"

The boy frowned. "Wot be ye talkin' about, cat whipper?"

"Why, Captain Goodacre, th' man ye jist wuz talkin' to there. He be captain o' th' *Rattlesnake*—th' privateer—an' a lucky ship it be wot with th' booty they gets."

The sweep stepped out of the shed and stared toward the tavern door until, some time later, he heard the cat whipper calling out impatiently that his shoes were finished.

17

❖

SEA STORIES

THE PINES cast a tangled network of shadows across the moon-washed sand of the road. The small figure of the sweep was alternately caught in the moonshine and then snuffed out by the shadows as he approached the charcoal pit. He carried the jug with one hand and his new shoes with the other. The hard-packed sand was smooth and cold under his bare feet. Ahead he could see the clearing, its stumps sticking up like rotted teeth, and the great dark hump of the smoldering stack. The hut stood low to one side, and the flickering cook fire winked at him through the brush as he approached. The dark, motionless figure of the charcoal burner stood like a statue, pole in hand, facing toward the road expectantly.

"That be ye?" he called hoarsely. "Tom?" he added.

"Aye, it be me," the boy replied.

A few minutes later he stepped into the weak glimmer of light cast by the fire. He put down the jug and set his shoes on a log nearby. He hunched down next to the flames. It was early November now, and the coming of winter was in the air.

"I see ye made it," the charcoal burner said needlessly.

"Aye. Fer certain," the sweep grunted. He glanced briefly at the bearded man from under his eyebrows. He reached into his shirt and pulled out a coin.

"Here be wot's left after buyin' th' shoes an' "—he waved a hand to the jug—"th' lightnin'." He held it out. "I wouldn't take none o' them paper Continentals in change."

The charcoal burner looked at the coin and scratched his nose reflectively for a moment. He shook his head. "Keep it fer yerself—it be yer pay. After all, yer not jist a bloomin' little black slavey."

"That be me good luck anyways," muttered the boy, putting the coin back. Then, looking at the bearded face that still peered expectantly into his own, it seemed right that he should nod his head and smile back.

There was a fresh pot waiting on the fire, and johnnycake. The charcoal burner stirred up the fire and sat watching him as he ate. He looked at the shoes and chuckled deep in his beard. "Be th' shoe leather too fine t' wear?"

The sweep swallowed and licked his fingers. "Th' leather be stiff an' has t' be eased up slow." He snorted in sudden mirth. "They does make me favor a duck flappin' down th' road, they be that big!"

The charcoal burner's chuckle rumbled into laughter. "Aye! I wuz thinkin' they reminded me o' a couple o' ore scows fer fair!" He slapped his knee. "Ye could walk on th' waters with them all right!"

His laughter dissolved into a series of coughs and snorts

and, when these passed, he smoothed out his beard and frowned for a time into the fire. He tipped the jug.

"An' I s'pose Sooy's wuz doin' a good business?"

"Aye." The boy told him about the recruiting party and Ben. The burner nodded. "Wars be strange—an' this one be stranger than most. There be jist as many fer th' king as agin him—an' jist as many as all o' them put together wot's fer themselves." He stirred up the fire. "An' why shouldn't Ben join th' army? He'll make a good enough soljer, if they teaches him t' tell the muzzle from th' stock o' his bleedin' musket. An' it don't matter if th' soljer boys don't know wot it's all fer." He upended the jug again.

The sweep wiped the food off his knife blade. "If'n I wuz a soljer, I'd want t' know fer sure wot I be fightin' fer—an' it better be fer me!" he grinned. "May not be so fancy a life but it be all I've got."

The charcoal burner rocked with laughter. "Ah, Tom, me boy! That be th' idee exactly. Ye puts yer finger square on it. That be all wot yerself an' me has got—a livin' body with two hands t' stick a gun in, an' them as wants th' blasted war is goin' t' use 'em. Only jist be sure t' sell as dear as ye kin—an' git a drop o' th' gravy." He controlled his sputtering laughter. "Th' army be a poor way t' use yerself: ye gits poor pay, bad livin' conditions, ye eats so much flour an' water yer guts turns t' pasteboard, an' yer liable t' end up dead. Fer someone else's idee. Now, them down at Sooy's has th' way. Stay clear o' the' blasted army—make cannon balls, charcoal even, or salt, if ye kin stand the blasted heat an' flies. Or, th' best o' it all, git yerself aboard a privateerin' ship. Yer not likely t' git hurt, not

if they kin help it! They be interested in prizes an' money, not bein' heroes." He got up and studied the stack. Satisfied, he settled himself at the fire once more.

"Privateerin'—aye, there's th' life!" He chuckled. "An' it be lawful too."

The sweep looked over at him, sprawled out over the sand, propped against a log like an old weather-beaten wreck. "Ye've been privateerin'?" He glanced at the cutlass, dangling in the hut.

"Ye don't think I've been makin' charcoal all me life, does ye? Ye thinks this"—he waved about at the scene—"ye thinks this be all Ol' John knows?" He snorted. "Aye, there be some here wot lives an' dies in th' blasted Pines—an' I may leave m' bones here too—but I've seen a bit o' this bleedin' world! I jist happened t' git washed ashore here, ye might say, by a bit o' bad luck."

He leaned far over toward the sweep. His eyes glittered. "Aye. I've done privateerin'—in every war till this here one, an' there's most always a war goin' on somewhere. An' between th' wars?" He winked ludicrously at the boy. "Well—ye knows wot they sez: peace makes pirates! Ye gits used t' th' life an' when th' fightin' stops ye jist sorta keeps on privateerin' fer yerself." He paused and studied the boy's face. "Ah-h—come on with ye!" He burst into a cackling laugh. "Be ye surprised t' meet a real live pirate? Aye! I could tell ye some stories!" He wiped his mouth and sat back up, rubbing his leg. "If'n I jist hadn't got in th' way o' th' shot." He looked about the pit. "Don't look like much o' a life now do it?"

The boy stood up. The charcoal burner reached for the jug and held it out to him. "Here—have yer sips an' sit awhile, Tom. I'll take yer time at th' stack."

The boy sat down. He took the jug, and his brow furrowed. Th' beard be lonely fer company—even fer a soot devil!

The charcoal burner combed his beard idly with his black-ened fingers and gazed at the dancing flames. He picked up a handful of sand and let it trickle out of his big fist.

"Ah, Tom, me lad," he began, "ye should have been with us in th' fifties." His eyes narrowed as he squinted back into the past. "Ye'd sail in t' th' islands after a spell o' th' dirty work. Th' water clear an' blue, an' th' green o' th' palm trees an' th' mountains—so purty ye felt like cryin'—an' th' air as soft as velvet, like it was heaven. An' mebbe it wuz! Aye, an' th' rum an' th' wenches an' ——"

His voice went on through the night hours, telling his tales of long ago.

18

A WAGON RIDE

NOVEMBER passed in blustery, wet misery, and December had begun the same. The charcoal burner and the sweep had completed the burning of two stacks. Twice they had sent the high-sided coal wagon lurching down the road, loaded with fuel for the furnace at Batsto. Now, once again they were extracting the charcoal from a stack.

The morning was dark and oppressive. A billowing fog laid a moist, concealing shroud all about, lending a dismal and eerie aspect to the steaming pit, and to the two figures working there.

They used long-handled rakes with iron teeth to remove the charcoal from the stack through a hole cut in its side. When the interior of the stack began to flame, they closed the hole and opened another. Occasionally the boy would stop raking and carry buckets of water from the stream to quench further burning in the freshly mined charcoal—and then further billows of steam were added to the strange scene.

The charcoal burner's puzzled eyes wandered often to the

boy, who plodded doggedly, silently about his work, his lips pressed firmly together. A curtain of sullen silence seemed to hang between them like the fog. Until the last few days the pit had been a different place—cheery, full of talk and jokes. The weather, the work, even the aching in his leg hadn't seemed nearly so bad since the sweep had arrived. Then the boy had seemed to slowly withdraw into a world of sulky moodiness.

Turning about now, the sweep's eyes passed over the charcoal burner—then jumped back to the man's face with a smoldering look. "Wotcha lookin' at me all th' time fer—does I have horns or somethin'?"

The sooty, bearded man straightened up, and for a moment they stared warily at each other.

"Jist takin' muster t' see if ye still wuz here is all—since ye've given up talkin'!" He pushed some pieces of charcoal into a small pile. "Ye'd almost think ye din't enjoy yer dooties or din't like yer shipmates—or that th' victuals wuzn't t' yer taste."

The sweep dumped a full bucket on a small chunk of glowing charcoal and flung it down. His eyes roved restlessly over the ground, to the charcoal burner, to the stack, to the faint gray silhouette of the the pines briefly revealed in the mists, and back to the ragged charcoal burner.

"A-a-ah," he growled, scuffing the sand. "Taint any o' that—it's jist that this blasted place be like th' end o' th' world almost. In th' city—Gilligan's even—there be people, an' th' fightin' an' foolin' an' hangin' around an' all."

The charcoal burner stroked his beard and nodded his head slowly. "Aye. O' course! I been sittin' in me cabin an' not givin' mind t' th' needs o' th' crew. Ye got t' take th' ship t' port now and then. Got t' head fer th' islands an' give yer crew a caper—or they gits t' fightin' an' bickerin' an' moonin' around." He studied the boy. "Lissen, Tom—why not jist take yerself t' Batsto this afternoon along with th' coal wagon? I kin clean up here an' have it ready fer buildin' th' new stack when ye gits back. Do ye good it will."

And so, at midday, when they had finished loading the wagon, the sweep washed up in the stream and raked his hair back from his forehead. He put the coins he had earned in a pouch and stuffed it in his shirt. As he joined the teamster sitting on the lazy board of the wagon, the charcoal burner ducked into the hut and reappeared, shaking the dust from an old ragged piece of fur. He tossed it to the sweep. "There be me coon hat, Tom. Ye kin hide under it if they looks too close at ye."

The boy put the mangy old fur cap on, and it covered his ears and most of his face. He grinned reluctantly, for the first time in days. "They'll be shootin' me fer a varmint I'm thinkin'."

The teamster cracked his whip over the teams' patient backs and the wagon lurched forward. The charcoal burner smiled crookedly and lifted a hand. "Be lookin' fer ye."

The bearded figure stood in the swirling mists, peering at their backs. He lifted a hand again before the wagon disappeared in the mist and the trees, then let it drop limply to his side.

The sweep had absently watched the lazy sway of the horses' haunches, studied the sandy road passing beneath the gently rocking wagon. He frowned. He turned around, lifted his hand, but the pit had faded from sight now. He fastened his gaze on the ears of the right lead horse. He felt vaguely uncomfortable and displeased with himself and didn't hear the teamster speak at first.

"I sez," the man repeated, "it must be a bloody relief—gittin' away from that one." He tapped his head meaningfully and winked at the boy. "Yer smart t' git out, 'fore ye're addled too —th' stories ye hears."

The sweep looked at the man, the heavy jowls, the pale eyes, his face much scarred by the pox. He looked away.

"Taint so bad."

"Then yer a queer one. Taint no one kin work with th' ol' buzzard. Crazy as a coot, sour as sin—can't keep his helpers—" he eyed the boy—"such as will try him." He cracked his whip and barked at the team. "Have t' be near th' end o' th' rope t' even try, ye'd think. 'Course, it be no business o' mine if ye wants t'bury yerself in th' woods with th' ol' devil. I'm not th' one t' go diggin' in t' reasons. Everyone t' his own tastes, I sez."

They were passing a vast burned-over area. The charred and tortured tree trunks that remained stood like black tombstones on the grave of the forest. It seemed to suit the day. The boy tried to picture the fiery holocaust that it must have been—the crackling of the pines, the smoke, the heat, the roaring. He looked at his hands, the soot ground into them, the black arcs under his nails.

"Ye hears all sorts o' stories," the teamster resumed. "Like him havin' been a pirate—on th' account as they say. Makes ye wonder if he might not have—ye know—a little somethin' hid someplace? Hey?" The man waited expectantly and grinned knowingly at the boy, who stared ahead. They rode on in silence.

"Well, like I sez, everyone t' his own tastes." He measured the sweep with his eyes. "Glad t' see that ye chose th' path o' hard work an' honesty. There be some—ye knows th' kind— who leaves th' city, fer one reason an' another, an' falls in with th' wrong bunch. 'Course ye've heard o' Joe Mulliner"—his small eyes flicked to the boy—"an' his gang, an' th' others like him. Refugees they calls themselves. An' bandits is wot they be. Thievin', burnin', killin', plunderin' all over the Pines." He peered about at the trees. "Burnt one o' Mr. Wescoat's buildin's jist this mornin'—full o' a prize cargo wot jist come up th' river. It's got so an honest, hardworkin' man can't go about his business. Aye. I tell ye th' Forks is in a state, they be that scared o' wot's comin' next."

The sweep sat hunched against the chill. He was glad to have the coonskin hat. His attention wandered. His thoughts returned to the charcoal pit. *Ye had t' do it din't ye? Like a babe cryin' fer a sweet—poutin' an' moonin' an' sulkin' around. Plaguin' th' ol' beard—him wot's helped ye.* He jammed a fist against a palm.

The wagon moved steadily through the corridor of green pines and oaks with their tenacious brown leaves still clinging wetly. Then briefly along the bank of a swift, twisting, copper-colored stream flecked with bubbles and foam, like a mug of hot mulled ale. Soon they could hear the pounding of the hammer and then they saw the smoke wisping into the low clouds above the trees.

The sweep sat erect with anticipation. He smiled, remembering his first awestruck sight of Batsto. It seemed a long, long time ago.

The team rattled to a halt at the furnace bank—next to a large coal storage shed. The teamster turned to the boy dourly. "Here we be. Yer sure not much in th' line o' company, I'll say that. I sez ye should stay with yer crazy friend in th' woods—ye makes a pair ye do."

The sweep paid no heed. He nodded his thanks and jumped to the ground before the man finished.

He stood on the bank and listened to the music of the strange orchestra. The roar of the furnace, the creak and splash of the water wheel, of shafts and cams turning, pumping the gasping bellows, the small human voices—and over it all the beat of the hammer that crushed the ore, lifting and dropping like a metronome keeping time for the gods.

He watched an ore boat being poled down the lake to the landing by the stamping mill. He looked at the piles of new pig iron, cannon balls, kettles, pipes, skillets—all kinds of ironware piled here and there. Nearby, burly men pushed handcarts over the walkway to the furnace top.

Aye—it wuz strange, the sweep thought, *how they done it. Heat up that reddish stuff he had seen 'em diggin' up in th' bogs with charcoal an' then*—he shook his head and smiled—*aye, an' then toss in some shells from th' shore an' let it all cook an' bubble an' ye opens that hole at th' bottom an', devil take*

*it, out runs th' iron! An' th' bellows pumpin' an' blowin' on th'
mess like ye wuz tryin' t' start a cook fire in th' rain! Aye—it
be some kind o' magic.*

He looked over at the rows of log cabins where the workers
lived. Behind him stood the store and the ironmaster's stone
house. Over near the dam the wheel of the gristmill turned
lazily.

He gazed at the surrounding forest and pictured in his mind
the activity hidden there. He thought of the ships at the landing, and the river leading to the ocean—and then he thought
of what lay beyond that.

He jammed his hands in his pockets and walked slowly
toward the landing at the Forks.

19

CAPTURE

H E HAD been foolish to come to the Forks. A wagon ride, a look at Batsto, a little purchase at the store and then a quiet walk back to the pit. That was the plan. But not to the landing where he had called such attention to himself, where there were those who were ready, hoping to do him violence.

And so here he was now, with his hands bound behind his back, being led off into the woods with a noose about his neck. Would he ever learn?

First of all, there had been the newspaper. The *Philadelphia Ledger*—a new paper put out by the Tories and the British. It had been tacked right there beside the tavern door.

One thing he could read for certain was Gilligan's name. He had studied those letters often enough on the faded sign that hung crookedly at the plasterer's door. Now his eyes had roved over the insane tangle on the sheet like a sailor in a storm looking out for rocks. The name had leapt out from the page. Ah-h! An' wot did it say—all them other little hen scratches above th' name? As if he didn't know! Aye—an' din't he know

enough o' wot it had t' say t' jist turn around an' leave? Ah—
but it ain't every day ye kin read from yer own tombstone—
in a manner o' speakin'.

He had waited patiently—waited until a stooped, kindly,
harmless-looking old man with spectacles had stopped to read
the paper. The sweep had looked about and then tugged gently
at the man's sleeve. "Would ye be so kind, sir, t' read"—he
pointed to the little box of words—"them words there t' me?"

The old man had nodded vaguely. The sweep stood on a
chair and listened as the old man had bent close to the sheet
and read them to him in a quavering voice.

RUN AWAY FROM THE SUBSCRIBER, IN PHILADELPHIA, ON
THE 26TH DAY OF SEPTEMBER LAST, A CHIMNEY SWEEP
NAMED JACK JONES—SOMETIMES CALLS HIMSELF TOM FRY;
OF SMALL STATURE, OF FAIR COMPLEXION WHEN CLEAN BUT
USUALLY WEARS A DIRTY FACE; BROWN HAIR, DARK EYES;
HE IS A CLEVER, IMPUDENT FELLOW, MUCH GIVEN TO GAM-
ING. HAD ON WHEN HE WENT AWAY A BLUE HOMESPUN
COAT AND LEATHER BREECHES, SOMEWHAT WORN AND
SOOTY. WHOEVER TAKES UP SAID SWEEP AND SECURES HIM
SO THAT HIS MASTER MAY GET HIM AGAIN SHALL HAVE THE
SUM OF FIVE DOLLARS (SILVER) REWARD AND IF BROUGHT
HOME, REASONABLE CHARGES—BY PATRICK GILLIGAN.

The old man had frowned, fingered his chin and then peered
down at the boy through his spectacles. "Hm-m. Be that you
me lad?"

The sweep jumped from the chair and pulled the fur hat

tightly down about his face. "No!" He shook his head and looked nervously about. "No. Thank ye kindly but that be someone else—aye, someone else wot I be—uh—lookin' fer."

He had drifted away, into a group of sailors, and had left the old man leaning on his crooked cane, still scratching his chin, squinting about absently.

Ah, now it was time to leave for certain! How many others, with better eyes, had read that? How many indeed? He looked down at his coat—faded, but still, without doubt, blue, as the printed words had said. He felt about 10 feet tall—like a light-house for all to steer to. "An' why," the sweep muttered, "why did th' ol' sot o' a soot peddler have t' put in that about th' gamin'?"

He had gotten a grip on himself. He would walk as quietly and as calmly as he could through the busy settlement to the Batsto road, and when he reached Batsto he would continue right past and he wouldn't stop until he reached the charcoal pit. Well—perhaps he would stop at Sooy's and get a jug for the beard, and some molasses. But he was not a complete dunce— he could read the cards—and he knew when it was time to lay them down, cut his losses and leave.

He had walked quite nonchalantly, he had thought, the length of the street, with its nondescript collection of taverns, stores and warehouses—and ships—oh yes, the ships! He had relaxed. "Five silver dollars, Tom. Din't know Gilligan set sich a store on ye. No sixpence reward fer you!"

He had been smart, he thought, not to take any more chances. He probably could have stayed and none the wiser. Who would think of taking him back through the British lines?

He looked back again at the ships, the piles of cargo stacked about, the sailors, the wagons loading. He had smiled at the group of four men who sauntered along behind him, and they had smiled and waved back in a friendly fashion.

He neared the last buildings of the village. The men behind naturally walked a bit faster than he did, and their crunching footsteps came closer until, as they were about to pass, they were all about him. He had looked up at them and smiled again, and they had smiled back again too. It was good to keep up a natural, confident appearance. They had walked on in this manner for a time—and then it had begun to dawn upon the sweep that they had now matched their pace to his. His heart had suddenly begun to race and a chill had swept

over him. You don't suppose? He had looked about again. No! They were not the kind he wanted to walk down that empty road with at all!

He had turned about abruptly and, smiling to the very end, had attempted to slip between them. "Jist remembered somethin' I have t' do fer me pa back t' th' landin'." A great hairy arm got in his way. As a matter of fact it picked him right up. "Me pa—th' captain o' th' ——" His voice rose until the kerchief was clamped roughly over his mouth. Another pair of

arms held his legs and a few moments later they had hustled him into the woods. His eyes had rotated wildly, then gradually settled on the arm that went around his chest. Of course. There, where the sleeve was pulled up, he could see the two nasty red welts, the two arcs of scarred flesh—and he could almost count the teeth marks. He twisted his head about far enough to see the hard face above him out of the corner of his eye. The man's malevolent, smoldering gaze had met his own from a distance of about six inches. His thin lips had parted in a hoarse growl.

"I been waitin' fer ye, Soot Devil. I knowed ye'd be payin' us another visit."

They had flung him face down on the pine needles and bound his hands behind him, and then slipped a loop of cord around his neck. His legs were held fast by two of the quartet, although he had long since given up the hopeless struggle. The powerful man who had held him stared down coldly at the boy. "Ye'd be a smart soot devil, when we let yer legs go, if ye' jist stand up and walk along with us quiet like." He gently tugged at the cord that encircled the boy's neck. "There be a hangin' knot there—an' if ye tries any more o' yer tricks, it would jist plain pleasure me t' snub ye up real tight." His hand had gone to the ugly scar on his arm. "If ye wuzn't worth silver money in Philadelphia, I'd run ye up a tree an' let ye flap in th' breeze like the bloody Union Jack."

So the sweep had gotten carefully to his feet, and they had set off through the woods—and now he ruefully looked back on the adventure. Would he ever learn? *Yer a soot devil—aye, an' yer worse—yer a runaway soot devil wot has a fancy about yerself. Aye—yer born t' run like a bloody rabbit.*

And run he did—trotting along with his eyes glued to the line that led from the man's swinging fist to his neck. He must not stumble, trip, fall back. His mind emptied of all thoughts except the concentration on keeping that line slack.

20

THE OUTLAW CAMP

THE SWEEP sat on the ground before a log lean-to, at the extreme end of a leg chain which tethered him to a corner post.

Before him bodies lay strewn about a small clearing, amid a scattering of broken bottles, jugs, bits of torn clothing and chicken feathers. Mouths gaped open, arms and legs were flung awkwardly about. Had it not been for the sputtering rise and fall of the snoring one would have thought that some disaster, some bolt from the heavens had struck the camp of the refugees. A pale December sun cast little warmth over the scene. Wavering strings of smoke climbed weakly from the remains of untended campfires. The sun was overhead before the camp began to raggedly rouse itself from its stupor.

A few feet to one side of the sweep was a cage woven of slender branches. From within it a single proud and angry eye glared. The boy peered about the camp with its random collection of rough log shelters—and then once more met the beady gaze of his fellow prisoner—a white rooster of great size, somewhat bloody and the worse for wear.

"I'll be thankin' ye not t' look at me like it wuz any bloody fault o' mine—yer troubles. If ye wants t' know th' honest truth, ye din't ever have a chance fer anythin' better, unless ye favors makin' a pot pie more than fightin'." Grinning, he grasped the chain and rattled it. "See, I be no better off than ye be yerself."

The rooster croaked hoarsely and turned his head to reveal the torn and bloody socket where his other eye had been.

The sweep turned away. "Well, maybe I be a wee bit better off in truth. But ye don't have t' show it all t' me agin. Ye don't have t' brag on it."

He watched as several men walked unsteadily to the stream and soaked their heads in the cool waters.

He addressed his companion again. "Chicken, I'm thinkin' we wuz th' only ones in th' Province o' New Jersey wot wuzn't seasoned silly last night. Aye! It wuz a night t' give a preacher bad dreams. An' them shootin' contests. They wuz jist as like t' hit Tom Fry or poor chicken as th' blasted target. I like t' plowed me a furrow hidin'—I wuz that scared. Them bullets whistlin' around—lookin' fer a place t' light. And th' fightin'."

The rooster croaked again and tottered weakly across the cage.

"Well, th' people fights is wot I wuz thinkin' of, chicken. But I own that yer a fine fightin' cock. Ye makes th' feathers fly fer fair. I could see that before ye wuz set loose in the pit with that pore red." He grinned toward the cage. "If that ugly one wot feeds me had listened t' me bettin' advice, he'd be a richer

robber today an' "—he stopped short and frowned—"an' that
do call t' mind that I could use some victuals fer certain." He
searched hopefully among his captors for the man, and then
his gaze settled back on the rooster. "Blast! Yer beginnin' t'
look tasty, chicken. I gives ye warnin'. I keeps seein' ye bubblin'
in a pot. I jist can't help it." He pulled the threadbare blanket
about his shoulders. He squatted there as he had for three
days now, absently observing the scene before him, nursing
the emptiness in his belly.

The fires were built up and pots hung. About 20 men milled
around them. Each was dressed in his own fashion from the
booty taken in their raids on the Forks and the isolated farm-
houses in the Pines. A strange mix of fine velvets, sashes, and
lace with buckskin, linsey and moccasins. And strange tongues
—guttural German, cockney English, flat-sounding Dutch and
some unknown to the sweep. Deserters from both armies, including several fiercely mustachioed Hessians. Tories who
had been tarred and feathered and driven from their homes,
debtors fleeing jail, thieves, swamp men, outcasts all.

Twice since the sweep had been dragged to the hideout he
had watched as they had armed themselves and left—to return
late at night, their shouts growing like an approaching swarm
of locusts through the swamp, laden with their booty. They
had cleaned their guns and knives by the leaping yellow firelight and then they brought out the bottles and jugs and the
dark woods echoed to their shouting and shooting. There was
the cockfight and betting, and then much fighting about the
betting, until at last they collapsed wherever they were at the

moment. On the day after it was a long time before anyone remembered the sweep.

Now, as the winter sun began to sink, his keeper—a broad beamed, red-eyed fellow called Plum—appeared with a trencher of food. He crossed his arms on his chest and spread his feet and watched the sweep as he ate. "Well, th' major sez it's back t' yer 'appy 'ome tomorra, Soot Devil." He nodded toward several loaded wagons.

The sweep continued eating.

"Aye, ye'll be part o' th' cargo." His face, its features much rearranged by brawling, grinned brokenly. "It wuz bad luck fer ye, Soot Devil, wot ye done t' th' major, chewin' on 'is arm like it wuz a fine joint o' meat. Gettin' away, a little scratch like you an' "—his grin widened—"an' some o' th' lads thought it wuz a pretty joke. An' Joe Mulliner an' 'is lads—always funnin' the major—tellin' one an' all. Th' major, 'e can't be laughed at, 'e can't. Aye, 'e wuz bound t' ketch ye fer ——"

He stopped. The major approached the cage. He fed and watered his rooster, as he did every day. He examined the bloody bird tenderly and talked gently to it, kneeling by the cage. Finally he stood and his gaze fell upon the sweep. "Soot Devil," he spat softly. He strode away.

The flattened, smiling face turned to him again. "Aye, well, I ain't got nuthin' agin' a soot devil meself—unless 'e gits t' takin' a fancy t' 'isself." He picked up the trencher and followed the major.

The sweep looked over at the cage. The rooster strutted about, bobbed down to the corn kernels, posed for a moment on one leg and cocked his head at the sweep, his red comb hanging rakishly to one side. He cut a contented figure.

"He gives ye a little sweet talk an' yer jist a happy bird again ain't ye? An' him wot puts ye in th' pit'!" He shook his head. "Ye'll end in th' pot yet, fer all that, when he's done with ye."

He retreated with his blanket to the deepest corner of the shelter, with its pile of pine boughs, in search of warmth. The fires of another night's revelry reflected redly on his face and were mirrored on his bright eyes. But his mind was filled with other pictures.

Gilligan's. He could smell the smells, see the sweeps and the man himself. And the chimneys.

He saw himself, two months off the boat, just out of his mother's arms, early on a gray winter morning in Philadelphia. He walked the slushy cobbles with Gilligan and an older sweep. Peacock was his name. With brushes and scrapers and blankets over their shoulder they had chanted the call "Chim-ney Swee-e-p, Chim-ney Swee-e-p!" Angry curses had rained upon them for disturbing the early morning peace. Then they had been hailed by a servant in a fine house on Front Street. There was the usual haggling over price. Then he, the new boy, had worked with Gilligan on one flue—a simple straight one. They had raised and lowered a bag of bricks from the top, then worked a rope of twisted corn vines up and down and used their long-handled brushes as far as they would reach.

Meanwhile, Peacock had climbed the kitchen flue, a twisting black hole, thick with encrusted soot. They had finished with their chimney and waited in the kitchen for him. But there was no "Sweep-O!" that day. Exasperated at the lazy sweep, Gilligan had sent the boy to the roof again to stir Peacock. But he wasn't there and didn't answer to his calls. They had lowered the bag of bricks to locate him. They had broken open a hole in an upstairs bedroom, and there he was. Jammed fast, covered with soot, dead of suffocation.

"Aye! Ye won't fergit that! Wuz his grave it wuz. Jist a bundle o' sooty rags it looked like. An' then ye seen his fingers —bloody an' raw t' 'th' bone from his scratchin'."

Absently, now, the sweep fingered the sooty warts on his face and neck—the leathery black lumps that remained on his elbows and knees. He heard again the endless coughing in the darkness as they lay in Gilligan's straw. He wandered the streets of Philadelphia, remembered their jokes, their games. Oh yes! The happy, carefree sweeps!

"Who wuz th' little dunce wot let 'em do that? Gettin' walked on gits t' be a bloody habit. Ye does th' dirty work o' th' world and ye gits stepped on fer thanks." He stared fiercely at the fire-lit scene before him.

21

THE ROAD

MORNING brought a heavy, slushy snow, carried by a raw wind. The three wagons creaked out of the refugee camp early. Plum, who drove the second wagon, said that the weather was good—for avoiding rebel patrols that tried to prevent supplies from reaching the British in Philadelphia. He had bound the sweep's wrists, dropped the noose about his neck once more and tied the end of it to the rear of the wagon. "It be a smuggler's day," he said.

They had been on the way an hour or so now. The sweep plodded on behind the endlessly turning wheels. A corner of the canvas cover before him flapped carelessly in the wind and revealed the contraband beneath. Barrels of sugar, bags of coffee, boxes of tea, puncheons of rum. There were kegs of limes to spice the drinks of Tory and Redcoat and bolts of fine cloth for their ladies—as well as a soot devil to keep their chimneys clean.

The wet snow clung damply to his head and eyebrows. The fur hat of the charcoal burner had been lost in the scuffle with the major and his men. His wrists were raw from his futile attempts to work free of his bindings. The tangled woods, within spitting distance on each side, taunted him with an impossible escape. A hot wave of despair passed over him. His hope seemed suddenly to collapse like a struck tent. Unbelievably his eyes began to brim over.

Plum's coarse laugh cut into his mood. "'E's cryin'! Blast if 'e ain't cryin' like a babe, th' soot devil!" Through the sweep's tears the grinning face wavered unsteadily. "Cryin' fer 'is dear mum, 'e is—an' I wot she's a bloody sweetheart fer fair—wot say, lads?"

A flash of fury instantly replaced despair. The sweep lashed out with his heavy shoes and with great satisfaction found Plum's shin—though he was nearly fetched up short by the noose for his effort. Immediately a heavy clout to the side of his head sent him reeling and stumbling, his head ringing. He blinked and shook his head until the rear of the wagon came back into focus.

"Ye prickly black devil!" Plum cracked his whip viciously near the seat of the sweep's pants. The laughter of the other men turned his face scarlet. He fumed off to the head of the wagon where he set about belaboring the team with his whip and curses until the throbbing vein in his forehead seemed about to burst.

When, some time later, he dropped back near the sweep again he had achieved a surly calm, and he merely grunted when the sweep said that he was sorry he'd kicked him, that his foot must have been bewitched—especially since he knew that Plum was the only one who could help him.

" 'Elp ye do wot, ye barmy black bug!"

The sweep looked quickly about, then turned back to Plum. "Treasure, Plum! Help me git th' treasure from back there is wot!"

Plum answered with a short burst of harsh laughter. But then his eyes roved over the sweep's face in an agony of doubt. Finally spitting contemptuously in the sand, he stamped off to the team.

He soon drifted back to the sweep, elaborately examining the boy's bindings, looking at him out of the corner of his eye. The boy remained silent. Plum fell in step with him. He coughed and cleared his throat.

"Yer ropes—they ain't too tight?" His fingers tested the noose about the sweep's neck and loosened it slightly. He permitted his hand to roughly pat the boy's shoulder in comradely fashion as he withdrew it. "No 'ard feelin's, Soot Devil?" He smiled and they proceeded in silence for a time.

"Drink o' water? Some lightnin'?" He mopped his brow with a kerchief and scratched his nose nervously.

The sweep shook his head.

"Ah—well—yer a rum lad. Said that t' meself when I first laid eye on ye. I said t' meself, if I could give th' lad an 'elpin' 'and in any way ——" He looked encouragingly at the sweep but still the boy said nothing—as if he was sorry he had said what he had.

Plum pressed his lips together in exasperation, glanced over his shoulder, and then leaned to the sweep's ear. "Ye said," he whispered helpfully, "somethin' about"—his flat eyes took on a luster—"somethin' about treasure, did ye?"

Smiling faintly the sweep looked up at Plum and, after some thought, nodded.

Plum expelled a great gust of air. "Ah-h-h! Well! Plum might jist be able t' 'elp ye, lad." He now remembered his duties and returned to the team. He refreshed himself from a bottle and seemed in no particular hurry to return and continue the conversation.

When he did return he was casual and offhand. "Yer treasure," he chuckled, "yer treasure ye wuz sayin'. Ye've got yer winnin's hid back there?" He jerked his thumb toward the forest behind them and grinned. "Ye must 'ave a nice little pile o' coppers from yer gamin'. Ye jist tell Plum where it be an' ye kin trust 'im t' fetch it fer ye next time we comes t' th' city so ye kin, ye kin —" His voice trailed off. The sweep's head was shaking vigorously.

"Plum!" He lowered his voice. "Plum, this be no pile o' coppers from gamin'! I said treasure, Plum—buried treasure— aye, pirate gold!" He held Plum with his eyes. "It be there— fer th' one wot has th' guts t' go git it!"

A whipping gust of snow swirled madly about them and the wagons. The man bent toward the boy, cupped a hand about his ear, and listened.

22

LEAVING AGAIN

THAT FIRST night on the road to Philadelphia, Plum and the sweep had headed back east through the snow. They had walked all night and, when morning came, they had left the road and plunged into a vast cedar swamp.

Plum, breathing heavily, called out again to the sweep. "Ye knows where yer goin'? Be it much further?" He was splashing heavily through the muck and slime underfoot, often to his knees. His eyes darted about nervously, first to the rear and then to the boy, as they had since he had lifted the noose from that scrawny neck and cut the bonds about the bony wrists the evening before.

It was strangely quiet in the swamp. The snow only sifted lightly through the green vault above, and the raw wind that had buffeted them on the road was a mere rustling overhead. The white flakes that penetrated the swamp silently disappeared in the still pools of brown water that shone about the tangle of roots of the low growth, or lightly coated the carcasses of fallen cedars. It was warmer here in the swamp, and many small sounds told of the animals that had found a winter shelter.

Plum nearly pitched headlong over a root and paused, panting, to regain his balance. "Ye'd best know wot yer doin', Soot Devil, or ——" The sweep turned around and gazed silently back at him. His face was empty of expression, as if Plum were merely another cedar stump. He looked about, taking his bearings.

Plum licked his lips. His blunt fingers touched the pistol at his belt. His dull eyes narrowed, flickered for a moment with the dawning of an unpleasant thought.

The sweep resumed his progress through the swamp. As he

had found before, what supported him often collapsed beneath the burly Plum, who made heavy weather of it.

And later, when he heard cursing and splashing behind him he did not stop. "Soot Devil!" He heard struggling, sucking sounds. " 'Old on there, ye cheatin' Soot Devil." There was an edge of panic in the voice. "Not so bloody fast, ye hear! Lend me a 'and, mate!"

The sweep's lips pressed firmly together and he stepped up his pace through the tangle. The angry cries behind him grew fainter. A wild shot from Plum's pistol echoed through the swamp.

Sometime later the boy paused, leaning against a tree and listened. He was alone. He gingerly felt the rawness where the noose had chafed, smiled grimly and plunged on. "Th' beard 'll use his bloody blade on me like pore Ben if I don't git back an' help him build th' stack!"

By the time he was approaching the charcoal pit that evening the snow had stopped and several inches lay on the ground. In the bright moonlight he could see the hut, with the fire flickering warmly before it. Off to the side was the unmistakable bulk of the stack. The sweep frowned, puzzled. A dark figure appeared from behind it and moved toward the fire. The exhausted sweep quickened his pace. "Hullo!" he called out. The figure turned toward him. "It be me—Tom! I come as fast as ——" He stopped abruptly. The man was not the limping, bearded old charcoal burner. He looked to the hut where another strange face had emerged to look out at him by the firelight.

"Where be Ol' John—th' burner?"

The man dropped his pole and held his hands over the flames and peered at the sweep. "Could give ye a good guess, aye, a good guess." They both snickered. "An' who be yerself?"

"I be his helper."

"Ye *wuz* his helper is wot ye mean. *We* be burnin' th' coal here now." He looked sharply at the sweep. "He's dead—as if ye din't know that. Wot brings ye here?"

"Aye, an' who knows wot brings him here!" the one in the hut burst out. "Think on it—he left the day before, an' there wasn't no sign o' him when they found th' old pirate. Come back like a bloody vulture, I sez, t' find wot him an' his friends couldn't find tother night. I talked t' that scarfaced one wot drives th' coal wagon. He sez he could tell th' little soot devil wuz up t' no good, goin' t' git his refugee friends. Said he wuz talkin' 'bout treasure. Had th' greed in his eye, he said."

The sweep stared down at the fire. "Wot happened?"

The first man stood up and grasped his pole. "There ain't nuthin' left here. If ye has yer refugee friends with ye, tell 'em there ain't nuthin' here. Mr. Ball sent us out t' burn th' last stack 'fore th' furnace is shut down 'cuz o' th' wheel freezin'." He looked at the sweep with repugnance. "He cut up a couple fore they done him in—th' old buzzard."

The sweep looked about the pit. The smoke rose lazily from the stack. The same pot hung over the fire, and before it was the same log that the old charcoal burner had sat on. There were the same robes in the hut, and the jug. *Aye*, he thought, *it wuz a snug berth.* He pushed at the dirty sand with his foot.

The two strangers looked coldly at him.

The sweep turned and walked away from the pit.

"Why don't ye go back t' th' city where ye come from, Soot Devil?" one of them flung at the sweep's back.

The boy hunched his shoulders, jammed his hands into his pockets and took the road to Sooy's.

By the time the dim lights of the tavern showed through the pines he was stiff with the cold and his legs dragged heavily. He entered the crowded, smoky room and sat quietly in a dimly lit corner. The heat from the great fireplace replaced his shivering with a feverish warmth, and he dozed off with his head on his chest.

He woke with a start when the proprietor tapped insistently on his chair with a tray and asked unsmilingly for his order. The sweep's pockets were empty. He stood up, and presently he drifted across the room toward the door. He seemed to stumble over something that caused him to bump heavily against a tipsy ironworker. They nearly collapsed to the floor together.

"I begs yer pardon—I be a clumsy lil' dunce fer certain." He apologized profusely, fumbled and brushed at the man's coat as they regained their footing. His hand found its way expertly into a pocket and removed several coins.

When he slipped out of the door, a half-eaten joint of pork had disappeared under his coat and a handful of crumbling johnnycake had gone into his pocket along with the coins.

The road to Clamtown and Chestnut Neck on the coast stretched out like a white carpet between the pines. The branches of the trees were heavily laden with the wet snow.

Glancing back over his shoulder from time to time and
biting hungrily into the meat, the sweep scuffed along through
the untrodden snow.

23

CAPTAIN GOODACRE

ETWEEN voyages, when the *Rattlesnake* was anchored in
the Mullica River off Chestnut Neck, Captain Goodacre
conducted most of his business ashore, in the warmth and comfort of Payne's Tavern.

The little village swarmed with sailors from the privateers
and with the shipwrights who fitted them out for their destructive raids on British shipping. Boisterous teamsters loaded
captured cargoes in wagons for the risky trip through the Pines
to the Delaware. Hopefully, some of it would find its way to
Valley Forge where Washington's troops were suffering through
the grim winter months. The owners of the privateers, and
those who came in their carriages through the Pines to bid at
the auctions for the captured cargoes and ships, savored the
seafood—the clams and oysters and such that the bays were
noted for. They conferred earnestly with their captains over
tankards of ale or glasses of fine wines and rum from the
islands, and examined the cargoes that stuffed the warehouses.
Laborers from the nearby saltworks, swamp men, the usual

rough crowd of adventurers filled the town and its taverns to overflowing.

As the captain sat now at a table before a frost-rimmed window on this January morning, he could see his trim little schooner swinging to the wintry gusts blowing over the river, doing a nervous dance with the other privateers and their captured prizes. The stream looped gracefully about through the low marshland and then entered the cold, slate-gray waters of the great bay. Snow squalls obscured the sandy, low-lying islands beyond that flanked the inlet from the sea.

Captain Goodacre returned the papers he had been studying to his first mate with a nod.

"It's a pity the business is so cluttered up with paperwork, Mr. Jackways. Surrounded on all sides by rules and regulations it seems. I'm glad to see that all the clerks and lawyers and desk warriors in the Admiralty Court have finally allowed that we did indeed officially and legally seize the infernal goods." He smiled and his purple scar bent. "Not that they were there to see." He sipped at his tankard of ale. He picked up an oyster from the bowl before him and deftly opened the shell with his knife.

"Though I do say, Mr. Jackways, it is probably just as well that they keep a weather eye peeled. It's bad enough as it is— the madness that's come over the business. They are hard put to keep a man in the navy, much less the army. Every lad's head seems full of notions of gold—half distracted and out of the way of working for money in other dull trades." He chewed thoughtfully and looked about at the crowded room and then at the ships in the river.

"Anything that floats, and, methinks, a few that can't, mounts a bow chaser and puts to sea." He wiped his fingers and mouth with a kerchief. "And I hear, Mr. Jackways, that there are more men—the ablest and best men too, I might add—in our privateering ships than General Washington can recruit to fight the British armies. And"—he smiled thinly—"we don't seem to give much thought to those poor devils, do we?"

Mr. Jackways looked down at the table. "Aye, captain." He passed over some more papers. "The cargo should fetch a handsome price. Mr. Ball, Mr. Westcoat, Mr. Clark—all here sir to make their offers, and others too. The crew shares should be right handsome ones for certain. Not"—he rubbed his nose and grinned—"that ye'll ever have trouble gettin' the best men for yer crew, captain—what with yer good name."

"My good name," mused the captain. "A good name seems measured by the pounds, shillings and pence that one can deliver."

"Aye, captain, they measures ye by that. But they measures ye also by how a fine, educated man like yerself, a captain who deals with the gentry, kin join the common hands fer their games and all—and is fair an' square when the ship goes off soundings too."

"A fair man and a patriot, Mr. Jackways, is what I wish to be called—helping the cause of freedom as best I can, helping to make a country of free and equal men."

Mr. Jackways remained respectfully silent while Captain Goodacre looked out of the window for a time. Then with a cough he rattled the papers before him. "The new crew is near complete, captain—signed and ready to weigh anchor next Thursday."

They bent to their work, checking and rechecking their lists. The ship's sails and rigging, the swivel guns, bayonets, cutlasses, boarding pikes, iron shot for the murderous, close-firing carronades, food to feed the crew and the captives—all the infinite details of planning for a successful privateering voyage must be carefully arranged for.

When the light of the short, sunless winter day began to fade, Captain Goodacre flung down his quill pen and wearily rubbed his eyes.

"Enough, enough," he sighed. "Time for a glass and victuals." He stretched and genially acknowledged the greetings of several other privateersmen. "And perhaps a game tonight, Mr. Jackways."

He looked out of the window. The ships were dark silhouettes now on the twisting gray path of the river. The windows in the handful of weathered, shingled houses that made up the settlement of Chestnut Neck glowed with candlelight. The figure of a small boy, bundled against the cold, passed briefly before the window.

Captain Goodacre frowned, turned back and studied his hands, fanned out upon the table.

"Ye remember the little soot devil, Mr. Jackways, that ye said applied as a powder boy? What seems to have become of him—is he seen about? That mite sticks in my mind like a burr, he does."

Mr. Jackways tapped a stack of papers into an even pile

and tied them up neatly with a ribbon. "Aye, captain. He seems to be workin' off an' on at the saltworks." He chuckled. "They be that hard put t' find workers fer th' vats that they take anyone fer th' nasty work and no questions."

He bent down to the floor to get his leather bag. "Aye," he continued, "he's known t' visit the Neck here now and again—and they say ye'd best keep a hand on yer money when he does. He has a light touch in a pocket they say, bein' a sweep, ye know. Ye wouldn't want him aboard, o' course." He tucked the last of the papers into the bag.

Captain Goodacre nodded absently. "They do seem to all follow the same poor path. But there was pepper in that little joint . . . perhaps . . ." He shook his head as if to dispel his thought, rapped his tankard on the table and looked about for the serving girl. A few minutes later he lifted the tankard to his companion but then set it down without drinking. For a time he gazed into the dim, smoky air of the tavern. "Perhaps we'll see about that lad," he said presently, ignoring the startled expression on his first mate's face. "A tough little scrap of a powder monkey he'd make," he said with more firmness. "Seek him out, Mr. Jackways . . . and we'll chance it that he leaves his light fingers ashore." The captain smiled and once more he raised his tankard.

"To another successful voyage, Mr. Jackways—and may it contribute in its small way to the success of General Washington."